Contents

CLARICE LISPECTOR

Near to the Wild Heart

Translated from the Portuguese by Alison Entrekin
Edited and with an Introduction by Benjamin Moser

PENGUIN BOOKS

PENGUIN CLASSICS

Published by the Penguin Group
Penguin Books Ltd, 80 Strand, London WC2R ORL, England
Penguin Group (USA) Inc., 375 Hudson Street, New York, New York 10014, USA
Penguin Group (Canada), 90 Eglinton Avenue East, Suite 700, Toronto, Ontario,
Canada M4P 2Y3 (a division of Pearson Penguin Canada Inc.)
Penguin Ireland, 25 St Stephen's Green, Dublin 2, Ireland (a division of Penguin Books Ltd)
Penguin Group (Australia), 707 Collins Street, Melbourne, Victoria 3008, Australia
(a division of Pearson Australia Group Pty Ltd)
Penguin Books India Pvt Ltd, 11 Community Centre, Panchsheel Park,
New Delhi – 110 017, India
Penguin Group (NZ), 67 Apollo Drive, Rosedale, Auckland 0632, New Zealand
(a division of Pearson New Zealand Ltd)
Penguin Books (South Africa) (Pty) Ltd, Block D, Rosebank Office Park,
181 Jan Smuts Avenue, Parktown North, Gauteng 2193, South Africa

Penguin Books Ltd, Registered Offices: 80 Strand, London WC2R ORL, England

www.penguin.com

Originally published as *Perto do coraçao selvagem*. Published by arrangement with the
Heirs of Clarice Lispector and Agencia Literaria Carmen Balcells, Barcelona.
First published in the United States of America by New Directions Publishing
Corporation 2012
Published in Penguin Classics 2014
001

Printed in Great Britain by Clays Ltd, St Ives plc

978-0-141-19734-0

www.greenpenguin.co.uk

MIX
Paper from
responsible sources
FSC www.fsc.org   FSC™ C018179

Penguin Books is committed to a sustainable
future for our business, our readers and our planet.
This book is made from Forest Stewardship
Council™ certified paper.

Hurricane Clarice

FROM THE MOMENT OF HER BIRTH, IN THE WESTERN Ukrainian province of Podolia, amidst the racial war that killed her mother and grandfather and exiled her family to distant Brazil, Clarice Lispector had a difficult—often dramatically difficult—life. When I was writing my biography, *Why This World*, I naturally wished that it had been otherwise. I wished that there had been more episodes like the ovation that greeted *Near to the Wild Heart*, the book she published as an unknown twenty-three year old, in 1943.

When Clarice began writing, in March 1942, she was still in law school and still working as a journalist. In February she had transferred to the newspaper *A Noite*, once one of the glories of Brazilian journalism but then, under the dictatorship of Getúlio Vargas, a middling government organ.

She turned to her colleague Francisco de Assis Barbosa for help with the novel she had begun writing. "Groping in the darkness," she pieced the book together by jotting down her ideas in a notebook whenever they occurred to her. To concentrate, she quit the tiny maid's room in the apartment she shared with her sisters and brother-in-law and spent a month in a nearby boardinghouse, where she worked intensely. At length the book took shape, but she feared it was more a pile of notes than a full-fledged novel. Her first love, the writer Lúcio Cardoso, whose homosexuality doomed the relationship, assured her that the fragments were a book in themselves. Barbosa read the originals chapter by chapter, but Clarice rejected his occasional suggestions with characteristic vividness: "When I reread what I've written," she told him, "I feel like I'm swallowing my own vomit."

Lúcio suggested a title, borrowed from James Joyce's *Portrait of the Artist as a Young Man*: "He was alone. He was unheeded, happy, and near to the wild heart of life." This became the book's epigraph, which, together with the occasional use of the stream-of-consciousness method, led certain critics to describe the book as Joycean. The comparison annoyed Clarice. "I discovered the quote, the title of the book, and Joyce himself once the book was already finished. I wrote it in eight or nine months, while I was studying, working, and getting engaged—but the book has no direct influence from my studies, my engagement, Joyce, or my work."

Barbosa, who together with Lúcio was one of the book's first readers, recalled his amazement. "As I devoured the chapters the author was typing, it slowly dawned on me that this was an extraordinary literary revelation," he said. "The excitement of Clarice, hurricane Clarice." He steered it to the book-publishing wing of their employer, A Noite, where it appeared with a bright pink cover, typical for books by women, in December 1943. It was not a lucrative arrangement for the new author. "I didn't have to pay anything [to have it published], but I didn't make any money either. If there was any profit, they kept it," Clarice said. A thousand copies were printed; in lieu of payment she got to keep a hundred. As soon as the book was ready she began sending the book out to critics.

"Everyone wanted to know who that girl was," the journalist Joel Silveira remembered. "Nobody had any idea. Suddenly everyone was talking about it." The reviews still bear witness to the excitement "hurricane Clarice" unleashed among the Brazilian intelligentsia. For almost a year after publication, articles about the book appeared continuously in every major city in Brazil. Sixteen years later a journalist wrote, "We have no memory of a more sensational debut, which lifted to such prominence a name that, until shortly before, had been completely unknown."

Clarice Lispector, critics wrote, was "the rarest literary personality in our world of letters"; "something exceptional;" possessed of a "bewildering verbal richness." "The whole book is a miracle of balance, perfectly engineered," combining the "intellectual lucidity of the characters of Dostoevsky with the purity of a child." In October 1944 the book won the prestigious Graça Aranha Prize for the best debut novel of 1943. The prize was a confirmation of what the *Folha Carioca* had discovered earlier that year when it asked its readers to elect the best novel of 1943. *Near to the Wild Heart* won with 457 votes. Considering that only nine hundred copies had actually been put on sale, it was a spectacular number. But it was appropriate to a book *A Manhã* declared to be "the greatest debut novel a woman had written in all of Brazilian literature." Another critic went further: "*Near to the Wild Heart* is the greatest novel a woman has ever written in the Portuguese language."

The author of the last statement, the young poet Lêdo Ivo, sought her out after reading the book. "I met Clarice Lispector at the exact moment that she published *Near to the Wild Heart*," he remembered. "The meeting took place in a restaurant in Cinelândia. We had lunch and our conversation strayed from literary matters. . . . The least I can say is that she was stunning. It was autumn, the leaves in the square were falling, and the grayness of the day helped underscore the beauty and luminosity of Clarice Lispector. Alongside the foreign climate was that strange voice, the guttural diction which rings in my ears to this day. I was not yet twenty years old—and, under the impact of her book, felt that I was standing before Virginia Woolf or Rosamund Lehmann."

The book's "strange voice," the "foreign climate" of its unusual language, made the deepest impression on its early readers. It did have certain points of resemblance with earlier Brazilian writing. "Clarice Lispector's work appears in our literary world as the most serious attempt at the introspective novel," wrote the dean of São Paulo critics, Sérgio Milliet. "For the first time, a Brazilian author goes beyond simple approximation in this almost virgin field of our literature; for the first time, an author penetrates the depths of the psychological complexity of the modern soul." But the affinity with other "introspective" writers, even those as close to her as Lúcio Cardoso, was superficial, as another prominent critic realized when writing that Clarice Lispector had "shifted the center of gravity around which the Brazilian novel had been revolving for about twenty years."

It is remarkable how rarely critics compared the work to that of any other Brazilian writer. Instead, they mentioned Joyce, Virginia Woolf, Katherine Mansfield, Dostoevsky, Proust, Gide, and Charles Morgan. This was not simply because the entire question of Brazil, that "certain instinct of nationality" Machado de Assis considered to be the heart of Brazilian literature, is absent from *Near to the Wild Heart*. It was that its language did not sound Brazilian. Lêdo Ivo, remembering

Clarice's "strange voice" and "guttural diction," writes, "Clarice Lispector was a foreigner. . . . The foreignness of her prose is one of the most overwhelming facts of our literary history, and even of the history of our language."

Later this language would be naturalized as that of a great Brazilian writer. But for the time being it sounded exotic. "In Brazil we see a certain stylistic conformity," wrote Antonio Candido, criticizing those writers who, whatever their other merits, think "that the generous impulse that inspires them is more important than the roughness of their material." And Sérgio Milliet noted that the wonder of the book was the author's achievement of "the precious and precise harmony between expression and substance."

This is the core of the fascination of *Near to the Wild Heart*, and of Clarice Lispector. It was not a matter of style versus substance, nor a simple question of emphasis, that separated her from those writers for whom "the generous impulse that inspires them is more important than the roughness of their material." It was a fundamentally different conception of art. In that first book she summed up the impulse Candido and Milliet sensed when she wrote, "You see, vision consisted of surprising the symbol of the thing in the thing itself." The remark was important enough for her to repeat it a hundred pages later—"the symbol of the thing in the thing itself"—and was the heart of her entire artistic project.

But as the phrase suggests, that project was less artistic than spiritual. The possibility of uniting a thing and its symbol, of reconnecting language to reality, and vice versa, is not an intellectual or artistic endeavor. It is instead intimately connected to the sacred realms of sexuality and creation. A word does not describe a preexisting thing but actually *is* that thing, or a word that *creates* the thing it describes: the search for that mystic word, the "word that has its own light," is the search of a lifetime. That search was an urgent preoccupation of centuries of Jewish mystics. Just as God, in Clarice's writing, is utterly devoid of any moral meaning, so does language signify nothing beyond what it expresses: "the symbol of the thing in the thing itself."

The unprecedented ovation that greeted Clarice Lispector's debut was also the beginning of the legend of Clarice Lispector, a tissue of rumors, mysteries, conjectures, and lies that in the public mind became inseparable from the woman herself. In 1961 a magazine reporter wrote, "There is a great curiosity surrounding the person of Clarice. She seldom appears in literary circles, avoids television programs and autograph sessions, and only a few rare people have been lucky enough to talk to her. 'Clarice Lispector doesn't exist,' some say. 'It's the pseudonym of someone who lives in Europe.' 'She's a beautiful woman,' claim others. 'I don't know her,' says a third. 'But I think she's a man. I've heard he's a diplomat.'"

The beginning of this legend can be dated to Sérgio Milliet's influential essay of January 1944, when he noted the oddness of the author's "strange and even unpleasant name, likely a pseudonym." When she read the article, Clarice wrote Milliet to thank him for his warm review, and to clear up the matter of her name. "I was prepared, I don't know why especially, for an acid beginning and a solitary end. Your words disarmed me. I suddenly even felt uneasy at being so well received. I who didn't expect to be received at all. Besides, the repulsion of others—I thought—would make me harder, more bound to the path of the work I had chosen. P.S. The name is really my own."

BENJAMIN MOSER
UTRECHT, MARCH 2012

He was alone. He was unheeded, happy, and near to the wild heart of life.

—James Joyce

Near to the Wild Heart

The Father ...

HER FATHER'S TYPEWRITER WENT CLACK-CLACK ...
clack-clack-clack ... The clock awoke in dustless tin-dlen.
The silence dragged out zzzzzz. What did the wardrobe say?
clothes-clothes-clothes. No, no. Amidst the clock, the typewriter and the silence there was an ear listening, large, pink
and dead. The three sounds were connected by the daylight
and the squeaking of the tree's little leaves rubbing against one
another radiant.

Leaning her forehead against the cold and shiny windowpane she gazed at the neighbor's yard, at the big world of
the hens-that-didn't-know-they-were-going-to-die. And she
could smell as if it were right beneath her nose the warm, hard-
packed earth, so fragrant and dry, where she just knew, she just
knew a worm or two was having a stretch before being eaten
by the hen that the people were going to eat.

There was a great, still moment, with nothing inside it. She
dilated her eyes, waited. Nothing came. Blank. But suddenly
the day was wound up and everything spluttered to life again,
the typewriter trotting, her father's cigarette smoking, the

silence, the little leaves, the naked chickens, the light, things coming to life again with the urgency of a kettle on the boil. The only thing missing was the tin-dlen of the clock that was ever so pretty. She closed her eyes, pretended to hear it and to the sound of the non-existent and rhythmic music rose up on tiptoes. She did three very light, winged dance steps.

Then suddenly she looked at everything with distaste as if she had eaten too much of that mixture. "Oi, oi, oi ..." she murmured wearily and then wondered: what's going to happen now now now? And always in the sliver of time that followed nothing happened if she kept waiting for what was going to happen, you see? She pushed away the difficult thought amusing herself with a movement of her bare foot on the dusty wooden floor. She rubbed her foot and watched her father out of the corner of her eye, waiting for his impatient and irritated glance. But nothing came. Nothing. It's hard to suck in people like the vacuum cleaner does.

"Daddy, I've made up a poem."

"What's it called?"

"'The Sun and I.'" With only a slight pause she recited: "'The hens in the yard have eaten two worms but I didn't see them.'"

"Well? What do the sun and you have to do with the poem?"

She looked at him for a moment. He hadn't understood ...

"The sun is above the worms, Daddy, and I made up the poem and didn't see the worms ..." —Pause. "I can make up another one right now: 'Hey sun, come play with me.' Or a longer one:

'I saw a little cloud
poor worm
I don't think she saw it.'"

"Lovely, darling, lovely. How do you make such a beautiful poem?"

"It isn't hard, you just make it up as you go along."

She had already dressed her doll, undressed it, imagined it going to a party where it shone among all the other daughters. A blue car ran over Arlete, killing her. Then along came the fairy and brought her back to life. Her daughter, the fairy, the blue car were none other than Joana herself, otherwise the game would have been boring. She always found a way to cast herself in the lead role precisely when events placed one character or another in the limelight. She was serious as she worked, in silence, arms by her side. She didn't need to be near Arlete to play with her. Even from a distance she possessed things.

She had fun with pieces of cardboard. She'd stare at them for a moment and each piece of cardboard was a pupil. Joana was the teacher. One of them was good and the other bad. Yes, yes, so what? What now now now? And always nothing came if she … there.

She invented a little man the size of her forefinger, wearing long trousers and a bow tie. She wore him in the pocket of her school uniform. The little man was truly sterling, a sterling chap, had a deep voice and would say from inside her pocket, "Joana, Your Majesty, would you be so kind as to lend me your ear a minute, just for a minute may I interrupt your busy self?" And then he would announce: "At your service, princess. Your wish is my command."

"Daddy, what shall I do?"

"Go do your homework."

"I've already done it."

"Go play."

"I've already played."

"Then don't pester me."

She twirled around and stopped still, watching without curiosity the walls and ceiling that spun and melted away. She walked on tiptoe only treading on the dark floorboards. She closed her eyes and walked, hands outstretched, until she came to a piece of furniture. Between her and the objects there was something, but whenever she caught that something in her hand, like a fly, and then peeked at it — though she was careful not to let anything escape — she only found her own hand, rosy pink and disappointed. Yes, I know the air, the air! But it was no use, it didn't explain things. That was one of her secrets. She would never allow herself to say, even to her father, that she never managed to catch "the thing." Precisely the things that really mattered she couldn't say. She only talked nonsense to people. Whenever she told Rute secrets, for example, she'd then get angry with Rute. It really was best to keep quiet. Another thing: if something hurt and if she watched the hands of the clock while it hurt, she'd see that the minutes counted on the clock passed and the hurt kept on hurting. Or, even when nothing hurt, if she stood in front of the clock watching it, whatever she wasn't feeling was also greater than the minutes counted on the clock. Now, when happiness or anger happened, she'd run to the clock and watch the seconds in vain.

She went over to the window, drew a cross on the windowsill and spat outside in a straight line. If she spat once more — now she could only do it again at night — the disaster wouldn't happen and God would be such a good friend of hers, such a good friend that … that what?

"Daddy, what shall I do?"

"I already told you: go play and leave me be!"

"But I've already played, I swear."

Her father laughed.

"But there's no end to playing …"

"Yes there is."

"Make up another game."

"I don't want to play or do homework."

"Well, what do you want to do?"

Joana thought about it.

"Nothing I know …"

"Do you want to fly?" asked her father absentmindedly.

"No," answered Joana." —Pause." What shall I do?"

This time her father thundered:

"Go bang your head against the wall!"

She went off making a little braid in her long, straight hair. Never never never yes yes, she sang quietly. She had recently learned to braid. She went over to the little table where the books were, played with them by looking at them from a distance. Housewife husband children, green for the man, white for the woman, scarlet could be a son or a daughter. Was "never" a man or a woman? Why wasn't "never" a son or a daughter? What about "yes"? Oh, so many things were entirely impossible. You could spend whole afternoons thinking. For example: who had said for the first time: never?

Her father finished his work and found her just sitting there, crying.

"What's this about, girl?" He picked her up, looked unfazed at her burning, sad little face. "What's this about?"

"I haven't got anything to do."

Never never yes yes. Everything was like the noise of the tram before falling asleep, until you felt a little afraid and drifted off. The mouth of the typewriter had snapped shut like an old woman's mouth, but it had all been making her heart race like the noise of the tram, except she wasn't going to sleep. It was her father's embrace. He meditated for a moment. But you couldn't do things for others, you helped them. The child was running wild, so thin and precocious … He sighed quickly, shaking his head. A little egg, that was it, a little live egg. What would become of Joana?

Joana's Day

THE CERTAINTY THAT EVIL IS MY CALLING, THOUGHT
Joana.

What else was that feeling of contained force, ready to burst
forth in violence, that longing to apply it with her eyes closed,
all of it, with the rash confidence of a wild beast? Wasn't it in
evil alone that you could breathe fearlessly, accepting the air
and your lungs? Not even pleasure would give me as much
pleasure as evil, she thought surprised. She felt a perfect animal inside her, full of contradictions, of selfishness and vitality.

She remembered her husband, who possibly wouldn't recognize her in this idea. She tried to remember what Otávio
looked like. The minute she sensed he had left the house, however, she transformed, concentrated on herself and, as if she
had merely been interrupted by him, continued slowly living
the thread of her childhood, forgetting him and moving from
room to room profoundly alone. From the quiet neighbor-
hood, from the distant houses, no sounds reached her. And,
free, not even she knew what she was thinking.

Yes, she felt a perfect animal inside her. The thought of one day setting this animal loose disgusted her. Perhaps for fear of lack of aesthetic. Or dreading a revelation … No, no, she repeated, you mustn't be afraid to create. Deep down the animal may have disgusted her because she still had in her a desire to please and to be loved by someone as powerful as her dead aunt. To then walk all over her, however, to disown her without a second thought. Because the best phrase and always still the youngest, was: goodness makes me want to be sick. Goodness was lukewarm and light. It smelled of raw meat kept for too long. Without entirely rotting in spite of everything. It was freshened up from time to time, seasoned a little, enough to keep it a piece of lukewarm, quiet meat.

One day, before she was married, when her aunt was still alive, she had seen a greedy man eating. She had secretly watched his bulging eyes, gleaming and stupid, trying to not to miss the slightest trace of flavor. And his hands, his hands. One holding a fork with a piece of bloody meat (not warm and quiet, but very much alive, ironic, immoral) skewered on it, the other twitching on the tablecloth, pawing it nervously in his urgency to eat another mouthful already. His legs under the table kept time to an inaudible melody, the devil's music, of pure, uncontained violence. The ferocity, the richness of his color … Reddish around the lips and at the base of his nose, pale and bluish under his beady eyes. A shiver had run down Joana's spine with the sorry cup of coffee in front of her. But she wouldn't be able to tell afterwards if it had been out of repugnance or fascination and lust. Both no doubt. She knew the man was a force. She didn't feel capable of eating as he did, being naturally reserved, but the demonstration perturbed her. She was also moved when she read horrible novels in which evil was cold and intense like a tub full of ice. As if she were watching someone drink water only to discover her own thirst, profound and ancient. Maybe it was just a lack of life: she was living less than she could and imagined that her thirst required floods. Maybe just a few sips ... Ah, that'll teach you, that'll teach you, her aunt would have said: never do it, never steal before you know whether what you want to steal is honestly reserved for you somewhere. Or not? Stealing makes everything more valuable. The taste of evil—chewing red, swallowing sugary fire.

Don't accuse myself. Seek the basis of selfishness: nothing that I am not can interest me, it is impossible to be any more than what you are (nevertheless I exceed myself even when I'm not delirious, I am more than myself almost normally); I have a body and everything that I do is a continuation of my beginning; if the Mayan civilization doesn't interest me it is because I have nothing in me that can connect with its bas-reliefs; I accept everything that comes from me because I am unaware of the causes and I may be trampling something vital without knowing it; this is my greatest humility, she figured.

Worst of all, she could scratch everything she had just thought. Her thoughts were, once erected, garden statues and she looked at them as she followed her path through the garden.

She was cheerful that day, pretty too. A bit of fever too. Why this romanticism: a bit of fever? But actually I do have one: eyes sparkling, this strength and this weakness, jumbled heartbeats. When the light breeze, the summer breeze, hit her body it shivered all over with cold and heat. And then she thought very quickly, unable to stop inventing. It's because I'm still very young and whenever I am touched or not touched, I feel—she reflected. Thinking now, for example, about blonde streams. Precisely because blonde streams don't exist, you see? and off you go. Yes, but golden flecks of sun, blonde in a way

… So I didn't really imagine it. It's always the same old pitfall: neither evil or the imagination. In the former, in the final center, the simple and adjectiveless feeling, blind as a rolling stone. In the imagination, for it alone has the power of evil, just the enlarged and transformed vision: beneath it the impassive truth. You lie and stumble into the truth. Even in her freedom, when she chose cheerful new paths, she later recognized them. To be free was to carry on after all and there again was the beaten track. She would only see what was already inside her. Having lost the taste for imagining. What about the day I cried?—she felt a certain desire to lie too—I was studying math and suddenly felt the tremendous, cold impossibility of the miracle. I look through this window and the only truth, the truth I couldn't tell that man, if I went up to him, without him running away from me, the only truth is that I live. Sincerely, I live. Who am I? Well, that's a bit much. I remember a chromatic study by Bach and my mind strays. It is as cold and pure as ice, yet you can sleep on it. My consciousness strays, but it doesn't matter, I find the greatest serenity in hallucination. It is curious that I can't say who I am. That is to say, I know it all too well, but I can't say it. More than anything, I'm afraid to say it, because the moment I try to speak not only do I fail to express what I feel but what I feel slowly becomes what I say. Or at least what makes me act is not what I feel but what I say. I feel who I am and the impression is lodged in the highest part of my brain, on my lips (especially on my tongue), on the surface of my arms and also running through me, deep inside my body, but where, exactly where, I can't say. The taste is grey, slightly reddish, a bit bluish in the old parts, and it moves like gelatin, sluggishly. Sometimes it becomes sharp and wounds me, colliding with me. Very well, thinking now about blue sky, for example. But above all where does this certainty of being alive come from? No, I am not well. For no one asks themselves these questions and I ... But all you have to do is be quiet in order to discern, beneath all the realities, the only irreducible one, that of existence. And beneath all these uncertainties—the chromatic study—I know everything is perfect, because it followed its fated path regarding itself from scale to scale. Nothing escapes the perfection of things, that's how it is with everything. But it doesn't explain why I get all teary when Otávio coughs and places his hand on his chest, like this. Or when he smokes and the ash falls in his moustache without his noticing. Ah, pity is what I feel then. Pity is my way of loving. Of hating and communicating. It is what sustains me against the world, just as one person lives through desire, another through fear. Pity for things that happen without my knowledge. But I'm tired, in spite of my cheer today, cheer that comes from goodness knows where, like that of an early summer morning. I'm tired, acutely now! Let us cry together, quietly. For having suffered and continuing on so sweetly. Tired pain in a simplified tear. But this was a yearning for poetry, that I confess, God. Let us sleep hand in hand. The world rolls and somewhere out there are things I don't know. Let us sleep on God and mystery, a quiet, fragile ship floating on the sea, behold sleep.

Why was she so burning and light, like the air that comes from a stove whose lid is lifted?

The day had been the same as every other and maybe that was where the build-up of life had come from. She had awoken full of daylight, invaded. Still in bed, she had thought about sand, sea, drinking seawater at her dead aunt's house, about feeling, above all feeling. She waited a few seconds on the bed and because nothing happened she lived an ordinary day. She still hadn't freed herself of the desire-force-miracle, since she was a girl. The formula was repeated time and again: feeling the thing without possessing it. All it took was for everything to help her, to leave her light and pure, fasting in order to receive the imagination. Difficult as flying and with nothing beneath her feet receiving in her arms something extremely precious, a child for example. Even by herself at a certain point in the game she lost the feeling that she was lying—and she was afraid of not being present in all of her thoughts. She wanted the sea and felt the sheets on the bed. The day went on and left her behind, alone.

Still lying down, she had stayed silent, almost without thinking as sometimes happened. She glanced about the house full of sunlight, at that hour, the windows lofty and shiny as if they themselves were the light. Otávio had gone out. No one home. And as such no one inside her who could have the thoughts most disconnected from reality, if they wished. If I saw myself on earth from up in the stars I'd be alone from myself. It wasn't night, there were no stars, impossible to see oneself from such a distance. Absent-mindedly, she remembered someone (big teeth with spaces between them, eyes without lashes), saying very sure of his originality, but sincerely: my life is tremendously nocturnal. After speaking, this someone would just sit there, quiet as a cow at night; moving his head from time to time in a gesture without logic or purpose to then go back to concentrating on stupidity. He left everyone dumfounded. Ah, yes, the man was from her childhood and together with his memory was a moist bunch of large violets, quivering with luxuriance ... Now more awake, if she wanted to, if she let herself go a little more, Joana could relive her whole childhood … The short time she'd had with her father, the move to her aunt's house, the teacher teaching her to live, puberty mysteriously rising, boarding school … her marriage to Otávio … But it was all much shorter, a simple surprised glance would drain all these facts.

It really was a bit of fever. If sin existed, she had sinned. All her life had been an error, she was futile. Where was the woman with the voice? Where were the women who were just female? And what about the continuation of what she had begun as a child? It was a bit of fever. The result of those days wandering here and there, repudiating and loving the same things a thousand times over. Of those nights living on dark and silent, the tiny stars winking up high. The woman lying on the bed, vigilant eye in the half-light. The hazy white bed swimming in darkness. Tiredness slithering through her body, lucidity fleeing the octopus. Frayed dreams, beginnings of visions. Otávio living in the other bedroom. And suddenly all the lassitude of waiting concentrating itself into a quick, nervous body movement, a silent scream. Cold then, and sleep.

The Mother

ONE DAY THE FATHER'S FRIEND CAME FROM FAR AWAY and embraced him. At dinnertime, Joana gazed aghast and contrite at a naked yellow chicken on the table. Her father and the man were drinking wine and from time to time the man said:

"I can hardly believe you went and got yourself a daughter ..."

Her father would turn laughing to Joana and say:

"I bought her on the corner ..."

Her father was cheerful and serious too, rolling up bread balls. Sometimes he'd take a large sip of wine. The man would turn to Joana and say:

"Did you know that pigs go grunt-grunt-grunt?"

Her father replied:

"You're not cut out for it, Alfredo ..."

The man's name was Alfredo.

"You haven't even noticed," continued her father, "that the girl's too old to play at what pigs do ..."

They all laughed and so did Joana. Her father gave her another chicken wing and she ate it without bread.

17

"What does it feel like to have a girl?" said the man, chewing.

Her father wiped his mouth with his napkin, tilted his head to one side and said smiling:

"Sometimes it feels like I have a warm egg in my hand. Sometimes, nothing: total memory loss … Occasionally it feels like I have a girl of my own, really mine."

"Girly, girly, pearly, whirly, twirly …" sang the man looking at Joana. What are you going to be when you grow up and are a woman and everything?"

"She hasn't the slightest idea about everything my friend," declared her father, "but if she doesn't mind I can tell you her plans. She told me that when she grows up she is going to be a hero …"

The man laughed and laughed and laughed. He stopped suddenly, took Joana's chin in his hand and while he held it she couldn't chew:

"You're not going to cry because your secret's out of the bag, are you, girl?"

Then there was talk of things that for sure had happened before she was born. Sometimes it wasn't really about the kind of things that happen, just words—but also from before she was born. She would have preferred a thousand times over that it was raining because it would have been so much easier to sleep without being afraid of the dark. The two men went and got their hats to go out, so she got up and tugged on her father's coat:

"Stay a bit more …"

The men glanced at one another and there was an instant in which she wasn't sure if they were going to stay or go. But when her father and his friend looked a little serious and then laughed together she knew they were going to stay. At least until she was tired enough to go to bed without the sound of rain, without the sound of people, thinking about the rest of the black, empty, hushed house. They sat down and smoked. The light started to wink in her eyes and the next day, as soon as she was awake, she'd go peek at the neighbor's yard to see the chickens because today she'd eaten roast chicken.

"I couldn't forget her," her father was saying. "Not that I thought about her constantly. A thought here and there, like a reminder note to think later. Later it would come and I never gave it too much consideration. It was just that slight, painless pang, an unpronounced ah!, a moment of vague meditation, then forgetting. Her name was ..." He glanced at Joana. "Her name was Elza. I remember I even said to her: Elza is a name like an empty bag. She was sharp, oblique (you know how, don't you?), full of power. So quick and harsh in her conclusions, so independent and bitter that the first time we spoke I called her crass! Imagine ... She laughed, then went serious. Back then I tried to imagine what she did at night. Because it didn't seem possible that she slept. No, she never let herself go ever. And even that dry color (fortunately the girl didn't take after her), that color didn't go with a nightgown ... I imagined she spent the night praying, gazing at the dark sky, keeping vigil for someone. I had a bad memory, I couldn't even remember why I'd called her crass. But not so bad that I forgot her. I still pictured her walking on sand, her stiff footsteps, her scowling, faraway face. The most curious thing, Alfredo, is that there couldn't have been any sand. Nevertheless the vision was stubborn and resisted explanations."

The man was smoking, almost lying in his chair. Joana scratched at the red leather of the old armchair with her fingernail.

"Once I woke with a fever, in the middle of the night. It's almost as if I can still feel my tongue in my mouth, hot, dry, rough as a rag. You know how terrified I am of suffering, I'd rather sell my soul. Well I thought of her. Incredible. I was already thirty-two, if I'm not mistaken. I'd met her when I was twenty, fleetingly. And in a moment of distress, out of so many friends (and even you, as I didn't know what had become of you), at that moment I thought of her. What the hell ..."

The friend laughed:

"Hell indeed ..."

"You have no idea: I've never seen anyone so angry at people, but sincere anger and contempt too. And so good at the same time ... dryly good. Am I wrong? It was me who didn't like that kind of goodness: as if she was laughing at you. But I got used to it. She didn't need me. Nor I her, it is true. But we were always together. What I'd still like to know, would give anything to know, is what she thought so much about. You, who knows me well, would find me such a simpleton compared to her. So imagine the impression she made on my poor, scarce family: it was as if I'd brought to its ample pink bosom—remember, Alfredo?—they laughed—it was as if I'd brought the small-pox microbe, a heretic, goodness knows what ... Whatever, I really hope the little one there doesn't repeat her. Or me, for God's sake ... Fortunately I get the impression Joana is going to follow her own path ..."

"Then what?" said the man.

"Then ... nothing. She died as soon as she could."

Then the man said:

"Look, your daughter's almost asleep ... Be kind: put her to bed."

But she wasn't asleep. It was just that half closing her eyes, letting her head fall to one side, was a bit like if it was raining, everything mixed lightly together. That way when she lay down and pulled up the sheet she'd be more accustomed to sleeping and wouldn't feel the dark weighing on her chest. Especially today, now that she was afraid of Elza. But you couldn't be afraid of your mother. A mother was like a father. As her father carried her down the corridor to her room, she leaned her head against him, smelled the strong scent that came from his arms. She said without speaking: no, no, no ... To cheer herself up she thought: tomorrow, first thing tomorrow see the living chickens.

The last sunlight trembled outside in the green branches. The pigeons scratched the loose earth. From time to time the breeze and the silence of the school courtyard reached the classroom. Then everything became lighter, the teacher's voice floated like a white flag.

"And he and his whole family lived happily ever after." Pause—the trees rustled in the garden, it was a summer's day. "Write a summary of this story for our next class."

Still immersed in the story the children moved slowly, eyes light, mouths satisfied.

"What do you get when you become happy?" Her voice was a clear, sharp arrow. The teacher looked at Joana.

"Repeat the question ...?"

Silence. The teacher smiled as she stacked up the books.

"Ask it again, Joana. I didn't hear you properly."

"I'd like to know: once you're happy what happens? What comes next?" she repeated obstinately.

The woman stared at her in surprise.

"What a thought! I don't think I know what you mean, what a thought! Ask it again in other words ..."

"Being happy is for what?"

The teacher flushed—no one was ever sure why she went red. She noticed the whole class and sent them off for their break.

The janitor came to call Joana to the office. The teacher was there.

"Have a seat … Did you play a lot?"

"A little …"

"What do you want to be when you grow up?"

"I don't know."

"Well. Look, I too had a thought." She blushed. "Get a piece of paper, write down that question that you asked me today and put it away for a long time. When you are big read it again." She looked at her. "Who knows? Maybe one day you'll be able to answer it yourself somehow …" Her serious expression faded, she blushed. "Or maybe it doesn't matter and at least you'll be amused by …"

"No."

"No what?" the teacher asked surprised.

"I don't like being amused," said Joana proudly.

The teacher flushed again:

"Fine, go play."

When Joana had reached the door in two skips, the teacher called her again, this time blushing down to her neck, her eyes low, shuffling papers on the desk.

"Didn't you think it was odd … funny that I told you to write the question down to keep?"

"No," she said.

She turned back to the courtyard.

Joana's Walk

"I GET DISTRACTED A LOT," SAID JOANA TO OTÁVIO.

Just as the space surrounded by four walls has a specific value, provoked not so much because it is a space but because it is surrounded by walls. Otávio made her into something that wasn't her but himself and which Joana received out of pity for both, because both were incapable of freeing themselves through love, because she had meekly accepted her own fear of suffering, her inability to move beyond the frontier of revolt. Besides: how could she tie herself to a man without allowing him to imprison her? How could she prevent him from developing his four walls over her body and soul? And was there a way to have things without those things possessing her?

The afternoon was nude and limpid, without beginning or end. Light black birds flew distinct through the pure air, flew without a single human eye watching them. Far off the mountain hovered bulky and closed. There were two ways of looking at it: imagining that it was far away and big, in the first place; in the second, that it was small and near. But at any rate, a stupid, hard, brown mountain. How she hated nature sometimes.

Without knowing why, it struck her that this last thought, together with the mountain, concluded something, thumping the table with an open palm: there! heavily. The green-grey thing sprawling inside Joana like a lazy body, thin and rough, deep inside her, entirely dry, like a smile without saliva, like sleepless, listless eyes, the thing confirmed itself before the unmoving mountain. What she couldn't grasp with her hand was now glorious and tall and free and trying to sum it up was useless: pure air, summer afternoon. Because there had to be more than that. A useless victory over the leafy trees, a nothing to do of all things. Oh, God. That, yes, that: if God existed, he would surely have deserted that suddenly, excessively clean world, like a house on Saturday, quiet, dustless, smelling of soap. Joana smiled. Why did a waxed, clean house make her feel lost as if she were in a monastery, forlorn, wandering its corridors? And a lot of other things that she also observed. If she could bear pressing ice to her liver, for example, she was run through by faraway, sharp sensations, by luminous, fleeting ideas and then if she'd had to speak she'd have said: sublime, with outstretched hands, her eyes closed perhaps.

"Anyhow I get distracted a lot," she repeated.

She felt like a dry branch, sticking out of the air. Brittle, covered in old bark. Maybe she was thirsty, but there was no water nearby. And above all the suffocating certainty that if a man were to embrace her at that moment she would feel not a soft sweetness in her nerves, but lime juice stinging them, her body like wood near fire, warped, crackling, dry. She couldn't soothe herself by saying: this is just a pause, life will come afterwards like a wave of blood, washing over me, moistening my parched wood. She couldn't fool herself because she knew she was also living and that those moments were the peak of something difficult, of a painful experience for which she should be thankful: almost as if she were feeling time outside herself, in a detached manner.

"I noticed, you like walking," said Otávio picking up a twig. "As a matter of fact, you liked to even before we were married."

"Yes, very much," she answered.

She could give him any old thought and in so doing create a new relationship between them. This was what she most liked to do in the company of others. She wasn't obliged to follow the past and with one word could invent a course of life. If she said: I'm three months pregnant, presto! something would come to life between them. Though Otávio wasn't particularly stimulating. With him the next best thing was to connect with what had already happened. Even so, under his "spare me, spare me" gaze, she would open her hand from time to time and let a little bird dart out. Sometimes, however, perhaps due to the nature of what she said, no bridge was created between them and, on the contrary, an interval was born. "Otávio," she'd suddenly say to him, "has it ever occurred to you that a dot, a single dot without dimensions, is the utmost solitude? A dot cannot even count on itself, as often as not it is outside itself." As if she had tossed a hot coal at her husband, the phrase flipped about, wriggling through his hands until he rid himself of it with another phrase, cold like gray, gray to cover the interval: it's raining, I'm hungry, it's a beautiful day. Perhaps because she didn't know how to play. But she loved him, that way of picking up twigs of his.

She breathed in the warm, clear afternoon air and the part of her that needed water was still tense and stiff like someone waiting blindfolded for a gunshot.

Night came and she continued breathing at the same sterile

pace. But when the pre-dawn light lit the bedroom softly, things emerged fresh from shadow, she felt the new morning insinuating itself between the sheets and opened her eyes. She sat up in bed. Inside her it was as if death didn't exist, as if love could weld her, as if eternity were renewal.

... The Aunt ...

IT WAS A LONG JOURNEY AND FROM THE FARAWAY scrub came a cold smell of wet vegetation.

It was very early in the morning and Joana had barely had time to wash her face. Next to her the maid was amusing herself spelling out the advertisements in the tram. Joana had leaned her right temple against the seat and was allowing herself to be lulled into a stupor by the sweet sound of the wheels, sleepily transmitted through the wood. The ground sped past under her lowered eyes, swift, gray, streaked with fast, fleeting stripes. If she opened her eyes she'd see each stone and it'd ruin the mystery. But she half-closed them and the tram seemed to go faster and the cool, salty dawn breeze blew stronger.

At breakfast she'd had a strange, dark cake — tasting of wine and cockroaches — that they'd made her eat with such tenderness and pity that she'd been embarrassed to refuse it. Now it weighed in her stomach and brought a sadness to her body that joined the other sadness — something unmoving behind the curtain — with which she had fallen asleep and woken up.

"This sinking sand is a backbreaker," complained the maid.

She crossed the stretch of sand leading to her aunt's house, announcing the beach. From beneath the grains of sand sprouted thin, dark grasses that twisted harshly at the surface of the soft whiteness. The blustering wind blew from the invisible sea, bringing salt, sand, the tired sound of the waters, tangling skirts between legs, furiously licking Joana's and the maid's skin.

"Dratted wind," muttered the maid between clenched teeth.

A stronger gust lifted her skirt up to her face, exposing her dark, muscular thighs. The coconut trees twisted desperately and the brightness at once veiled and violent was reflected in the sand and in the sky, without the sun having shown itself yet. My God, what had happened to things? Everything screamed: no! no!

The aunt's house was a refuge where the wind and the light didn't enter. The maid sat down with a sigh in the dismal entrance hall, where, among the heavy, dark furniture, the smiles of framed men glowed slightly. Joana remained standing, barely breathing in the lukewarm smell that came sweet and still after the pungent ocean air. Mould and tea with sugar.

The door to the inside of the house opened finally and her aunt in a robe with a large flower print launched herself at her. Before she could make a move to defend herself, Joana was buried between two masses of soft, warm flesh that shook with sobs. From inside there, from the darkness, as if she was hearing it through a pillow, she heard the tears:

"Poor little orphan!"

She felt her face violently pulled away from her aunt's bosom by her fat hands and was observed by her for a second. The aunt went from one movement to the next with no transition, in quick, brusque jolts. A new wave of crying broke in her body and Joana received distraught kisses on her eyes, her mouth, her neck. Her aunt's tongue and mouth were squishy and warm like a dog's. Joana closed her eyes for a moment, swallowed down her nausea and the dark cake rising up from her stomach with a shiver throughout her body. The aunt pulled out a large, wrinkled handkerchief and blew her nose. The maid just sat there, gazing at the paintings, legs slack, mouth open. The aunt's bosom was deep, one could plunge their hand in as if reaching into a bag and pull out a surprise, a critter, a box, goodness knows what. Sobbing, it grew, grew and from inside the house came a smell of beans mixed with garlic. Somewhere, no doubt, someone would take large gulps of olive oil. The aunt's bosom could bury a person!

"Leave me alone!" cried Joana sharply, stomping her foot, eyes dilated, body shaking.

The aunt leaned against the piano, taken aback. The maid said:

"It's best, she's just tired."

Joana was panting, her face white. She ran her darkened eyes around the entrance hall, harried. The walls were thick, she was trapped, trapped! A man in a painting stared at her from inside his whiskers and her aunt's breasts could spill over her, in dissolved fat. She pushed open the heavy door and fled.

A wave of wind and sand came into the hall, lifted the curtains, bringing a breath of fresh air. Through the open door, the handkerchief at her mouth covering her sobs and surprise—oh the terrible disappointment—for a few moments the aunt saw her niece's skinny, bare legs run, run between sky and earth, until they disappeared toward the beach.

Joana dried her face wet with kisses and tears with the backs of her hands. She breathed more deeply, still feeling the insipid taste of that lukewarm saliva, the sweet perfume that came from her aunt's bosom. Unable to contain herself any more, rage and repugnance rose up in violent surges and leaning toward a cavity between the rocks she vomited, eyes closed, her body painful and vindictive.

The wind was licking her roughly now. Pale and fragile, her breathing light, she felt it salty, merry, run over her body, through her body, reinvigorating it. She half-opened her eyes. Down below the ocean glittered in waves of tin, lying there, deep, bulky, serene. It was dense and choppy, coiling around itself. Then, over the silent sand, it sprawled ... it sprawled like a living body. Beyond the wavelets was the sea—the sea. The sea, she said quietly, her voice hoarse.

She climbed down from the rocks, walked weakly across the solitary beach until she received the water at her feet. Squatting, her legs wobbly, she drank a little sea. She rested there like that. Sometimes she half-closed her eyes, right at sea level and swayed, so sharp was the sight—just the long green line, uniting her eyes with the water infinitely. The sun burst through the clouds and the little sparkles scintillating on the waters were tiny fires flaring up and dying out. The sea, beyond its waves, looked at her from afar, quiet, with no crying, no bosom. Big, big. Big, she smiled. And, suddenly, just like that, unexpectedly, she felt something strong inside her, a funny thing that made her shake a little. But it wasn't cold, nor was she sad, it was a big thing that came from the sea, that came from the taste of salt in her mouth and from her, from herself. It wasn't sadness, an almost horrible happiness ... Each time she looked at the sea and the quiet twinkling of the sea, she felt that tensing and then slackening in her body, in her waist, in her chest. She wasn't sure if she should laugh because there wasn't exactly anything funny. On the contrary, oh on the contrary, behind it was what had happened yesterday. She covered her face with her hands waiting almost ashamed, feeling the heat of her laughter and her exhalation being sucked back in. The water lapped at her now bare feet, growling between her toes, slinking away clear clear like a transparent beast. Transparent and alive ... She felt like drinking it, like biting it slowly. She caught it with cupped hands. The quiet little pool glinted serenely in the sunlight, grew warm, slithered away, escaped. The sand sucked it in quickly-quickly and then just sat there as if it had never known the water. She wet her face in it, ran her tongue over her empty, salty palm. The salt and sun were shiny little arrows that were born here and there, stinging her, tightening the skin of her wet face. Her happiness increased, gathered in her throat like a bag of air. But now it was a solemn happiness, without the desire to laugh. It was a happiness where you almost had to cry, for God's sake. The thought came to her slowly. Fearless, not gray and tearful as it had been until now, but nude and noiseless under the sun like the white sand. Daddy's dead. Daddy's dead. She breathed slowly. Daddy's dead. Now she really knew her father was dead. Now, next to the sea, where the twinkling was a shower of water fish. Her father had died just as the ocean was deep! she suddenly understood. Her father had died just as one couldn't see the bottom of the ocean, she felt.

She wasn't worn out from crying. She understood that her father had ended. That was all. And her sadness was a big, heavy tiredness, without anger. She walked along the immense beach with it. She looked at her feet dark and thin like twigs against the quiet whiteness where they sank in and from where they rose up rhythmically, in a breath. She walked, walked and there was nothing to be done: her father was dead.

She lay belly-down in the sand, hands covering her face, leaving only a tiny crack for air. It grew dark dark and circles and red blotches, full, tremulous spots slowly began to appear, growing and shrinking. The grains of sand nipped her skin, buried themselves in it. Even with her eyes closed she felt that on the beach the waves were sucked back by the sea quickly quickly, also with closed eyelids. Then they meekly returned, palms splayed, body loose. It was good to hear their sound. I am a person. And lots of things would follow. What? Whatever happened she would tell herself. No one would understand anyway: she'd think one thing and then didn't know how to tell it the same. Especially when it came to thinking everything was impossible. For example, sometimes she'd have an idea and would wonder surprised: why didn't I think of that before? It wasn't the same as suddenly seeing a little notch in the table and saying: now, I hadn't noticed that! It wasn't … Something thought didn't exist before it was thought. Such as, for example: the mark of Gustavo's fingers. It didn't come to life before you said: the mark of Gustavo's fingers … What you thought came to be thought. Moreover: not everything thought began to exist from that point on … Because if I say: Aunty is having lunch with Uncle, I'm not bringing anything to life. Or even if I decide: I'm going for a walk; it's nice, I go for my walk … and nothing exists. But if I say, for example: flowers on the grave, presto! there's something that didn't exist before I thought flowers on the grave. It was the same with music. Why couldn't she play every piece of music in existence on her own?—She looked at the open piano—it contained all music … Her eyes widened, dark, mysterious. "Everything, everything." That was when she began to lie.—She was a person who had already begun, after all. It was all impossible to explain, like that word "never," neither masculine or feminine. But even so didn't she know when to say "yes"? She did. Oh, she did more and more. For example, the sea. The sea was a lot. She felt like sinking into the sand thinking about it, or opening her eyes wide to stare, but then she couldn't find anything to stare at. At her aunt's house she'd no doubt be given sweets the first few days. She'd bathe in the blue and white bathtub, since she was going to live in the house. And every night, when it got dark, she'd put on a nightgown, go to sleep. In the morning, coffee with milk and biscuits. Her aunt always made big biscuits. But without salt. Like a person in black looking for the tram. She'd dunk the biscuit in the sea before eating it. She'd take a bite then fly home to take a sip of coffee. And so on. Then she'd play in the yard, where there were sticks and bottles. But above all that old chickenless chicken coop. It smelled of birdlime and filth and stuff drying. But one could sit in it, very close to the ground, looking at the earth. The earth made up of so many pieces that it hurt one's head to think how many. The chicken coop had bars and everything, it would be her house. And there was also her uncle's farm, which she had only visited, but where she would spend her holidays from now on. She was getting so many new things, wasn't she? She sunk her face into her hands. Oh, scary, scary. But it wasn't just scary. It was like when someone finishes something and says: "I'm all done, teacher." And the teacher says: "Sit there and wait for everyone else." And you sit there quietly waiting, like inside a church. A tall church and without saying anything. Fine, delicate saints. Cold to the touch. Cold and divine. And nothing says anything. Oh, scary, scary. But it wasn't just scary. I don't have anything to do either, I don't know what to do either. Like looking at something beautiful, a cute little chick, the sea, a knot in your throat. But it wasn't just that. Open eyes blinking, mixed with the things behind the curtain.

Joana's Joys

THE FREEDOM SHE SOMETIMES FELT. IT DIDN'T COME from clear reflections, but a state that seemed to be made of perceptions too organic to be formulated as thoughts. Sometimes at the bottom of the feeling wavered an idea that gave her a vague awareness of its kind and color.

The state she slipped into when she murmured: eternity. The thought itself took on a quality of eternity. It would magically deepen and broaden, without any actual content or form, but also without dimensions. The impression that if she could remain in the feeling for a few more instants she'd have a revelation—easily, like seeing the rest of the world just by leaning from the earth towards space. Eternity wasn't just time, but something like the deeply rooted certainty that she couldn't contain it in her body because of death; the impossibility of going beyond eternity was eternity; and a feeling in absolute, almost abstract purity was also eternal. What really gave her a sense of eternity was the impossibility of knowing how many human beings would succeed her body, which would one day be far from the present with the speed of a shooting star.

She defined eternity and explanations were born as fatal as the blows of her heart. She wouldn't change a single term, such were they her truth. No sooner had they germinated, however, than they became logically empty. Defining eternity as a quantity greater than time and greater even than the time the human mind can sustain as an idea didn't allow you, however, to fathom its duration. Its quality was precisely not having quantity, not being measurable and divisible because everything that could be measured and divided had a beginning and an end. Eternity was not an infinitely great quantity that was worn down, but eternity was succession.

Then Joana suddenly understood that the utmost beauty was to be found in succession, that movement explained form—it was so high and pure to cry: movement explains form!—and pain was also to be found in succession because the body was slower than the movement of uninterrupted continuity. The imagination grasped and possessed the future of the present, while the body was there at the beginning of the road, living at another pace, blind to the experience of the spirit … Through these perceptions—by means of them Joana made something exist—she communed with a joy that was enough in itself.

There were many good feelings. Climbing the hill, stopping at the top and, without looking, feeling the ground covered behind her, the farm in the distance. The wind ruffling her clothes, her hair. Her arms free, heart closing and opening wildly, but her face bright and serene under the sun. And knowing above all that the earth beneath her feet was so deep and so secret that she need not fear the invasion of understanding dissolving its mystery. This feeling had a quality of glory.

Certain moments in music. Music was of the same category as thought, both vibrated in the same movement and kind. Of the same quality as a thought so intimate that when heard, it revealed itself. As a thought so intimate that when she heard someone repeat the slightest nuances of its sounds, Joana was surprised at how she had been invaded and scattered. She didn't feel its harmony any more when it became popular—then it was no longer hers. Or even when she heard the piece several times, which destroyed the similarity: because her thoughts never repeated themselves, while music could be renewed exactly the same as itself—thoughts were only like music in their creation. Joana didn't identify profoundly with all sounds. Only with the pure ones, where what she loved was neither tragic nor comic.

There were lots of things to see too. Certain instants of seeing were like "flowers on the grave": what was seen came to exist. Joana didn't expect visions in miracles or announced by the angel Gabriel, however. They surprised her in things she had already set eyes on, but suddenly seeing for the first time, suddenly comprehending that the thing had been alive all along. Thus, a dog barking, silhouetted against the sky. It stood on its own, not requiring anything else to explain itself ... An open door swinging to and fro, creaking in the silence of an afternoon ... And suddenly, yes, there was the true thing. An old portrait of someone you don't know and will never recognize because the portrait is old or because the person portrayed has turned to dust—this modest lack of intention brought on a good, quiet moment in her. Also a pole without a flag, upright and mute, erected on a summer's day—face and body blind. To have a vision, the thing didn't have to be sad or happy or manifest itself. All it had to do was exist, preferably still and silent, in order to feel the mark in it. For heaven's sake, the mark of existence ... But it shouldn't be sought since everything that existed necessarily existed ... You see, vision consisted of surprising the symbol of the thing in the thing itself.

Her discoveries were confusing. But this also gave them a certain charm. How to clarify to herself, for example, that long, sharp lines clearly bore the mark? They were fine and slender. At any given moment they stopped every bit as much lines, every bit as much in the same state as at the beginning. Interrupted, always interrupted not because they terminated, but because no one could take them to an end. Circles were more perfect, less tragic and didn't move her enough. Circles were the work of man, finished before death and not even God could finish them better. While straight, fine, freestanding lines—were like thoughts.

Yet other confusions. That was how she remembered child-Joana before the sea: the peace that came from the eyes of the cow, the peace that came from the recumbent body of the sea, from the deep womb of the sea, from the cat stiff on the sidewalk. Everything is one, everything is one ... she had chanted. Her confusion lay in the interconnectedness of the sea, the cat, the cow and herself. Her confusion also came from not knowing if she had chanted "everything is one" when she was still a girl, staring at the sea, or later, remembering. Her confusion didn't just lend charm, however, but brought reality itself. It struck her that if she clearly ordered and explained what she had felt, she would have destroyed the essence of "everything is one." In her confusion, she was the truth itself unwittingly, which perhaps provided more power-of-life than knowing it. The truth which, although revealed, Joana couldn't use because it wasn't a part of her stem, but her root, binding her body to everything that was no longer hers, imponderable, impalpable.

Oh, there were many reasons for joy, joy without laughter, serious, profound, fresh. When she discovered things about herself at the precise moment in which she spoke, her thoughts running parallel to the words. One day she had told Otávio stories of child-Joana from the days of the maid who knew how to play like no one else. She used to play at dreaming.

"Are you asleep?"

"Very."

"Then wake up, it's after midnight … Did you have a dream?"

At first she dreamed of sheep, of going to school, of cats drinking milk. Little by little she dreamed of blue sheep, of going to a school in the middle of the forest, of cats drinking milk from gold saucers. And her dreams grew more and more dense and took on colors hard to dilute in words.

"I dreamed that the white balls were rising up from inside …"

"What balls? From inside where?"

"I don't know, just that they were rising …"

After listening to her, Otávio had said:

"I'm beginning to think they might have abandoned you too young … your aunt's house … strangers … then the boarding school …"

Joana had thought: but there was the teacher. She had replied:

"No … What else could they have done with me? Isn't it great to have had a childhood? No one can take it away from me …" and at that moment she had already begun to listen to herself, curious.

"I wouldn't return to my childhood for a minute," Otávio had gone on absorbed, no doubt thinking about the days of his cousin Isabel and sweet Lídia. "Not for a single instant."

"Me neither," Joana had hastened to reply, "not for a second. I don't miss it, you see?" And at this moment she declared out loud, slowly, enthralled, "I don't miss it, because I have my childhood more now than when it was happening ..."

Yes, there were many joyful things mixed with the blood.

And Joana could also think and feel along several different paths at the same time. In this manner, as Otávio was speaking, although she had listened to him, she had stared through the window at a little old lady in the sun, grubby, light and quick—a branch quivering in the breeze. A dry branch where there was so much femininity, Joana had thought, that the poor dear could have a child if life hadn't dried up in her body. Then, even as Joana was answering Otávio, she remembered the verse that her father had written especially for her to play with, in one of her what-shall-I-dos:

> *Daisy and Violet were wont to natter,*
> *one was blind, the other quite mad,*
> *the blind one heard the crazy one's chatter*
> *and ended up seeing what no one else had ...*

like a wheel wheeling, wheeling, stirring up the air and creating a breeze.

Even suffering was good because while the lowest suffering was taking place she also existed—like a separate river.

And she could also wait for the instant that was coming ... coming ... and without warning plowed into present and suddenly dissolved ... and another that was coming ... coming ...

...The Bath...

WHEN HER AUNT WENT TO PAY FOR HER PURCHASE,
Joana took the book and carefully slipped it among the others,
under her arm. Her aunt went white.

Outside she chose her words with care:

"Joana ... Joana, I saw ..."

Joana glanced at her quickly. She remained silent.

"But don't you have anything to say?" blurted her aunt in a
tearful voice. "My God, what will become of you?"

"Don't worry, ma'am."

"But just a girl ... Do you even know what you did?"

"Yes ..."

"Do you know ... do you know the word ...?"

"I stole the book, isn't that it?"

"But, Dear Lord! Now I'm at a complete loss, as she even
confesses to it!"

"You made me confess, ma'am."

"Do you think it's alright ... it's alright to steal?"

"Well ... maybe not."

"Why then ...?"

"I can."

"You?!" shouted the aunt.

"Yes, I stole because I wanted to. I'll only steal when I want to. There's no harm in that."

"Lord help me, when is there harm in it Joana?"

"When you steal and are afraid. I'm neither happy nor sad."

Her aunt gazed at her in distress.

"My dear, you're almost a woman, soon you'll be all grown up … In no time we're going to have to let down your dress … I beg you: swear you won't do it again, swear, swear for the love of our heavenly Father."

Joana looked at her curiously.

"But if I'm saying that I can do anything, that …" Explanations were useless. "Yes, I swear. For the love of my father."

Later, as she passed her aunt's bedroom, Joana heard her, her voice low and interrupted by sighs. Joana pressed her ear to the door, in the place where the mark of her head was already visible.

"Like a little demon … At my age and with my experience, after raising a daughter who is already married, Joana leaves me cold … Our Armanda never gave us any trouble, may God preserve her that way for her husband. I can't look after that girl any more, Alberto, I swear … I can do anything, she told me after stealing … Imagine … I went white. I told Father Felício, asked him for advice … He shook with me … Ah, I cannot go on! Even here at home, she's always quiet, as if she doesn't need anyone … And when she looks at you it's right in the eye, looking down her nose …"

"Yes," said her uncle slowly, "the strict regime of a boarding school might tame her. Father Felício is right. I think if my brother were still alive he wouldn't hesitate to send Joana to a boarding school, after seeing her steal ... Of all sins, precisely one of those that most offend God ... Deep down what bothers me a bit is this: her father, negligent as he was, wouldn't have had a problem sending Joana to reform school even ... I feel sorry for Joana, poor thing. You know, we'd never have sent Armanda away, even if she'd stolen everything in the bookstore."

"It's different! It's different!" exploded the aunt victoriously. "Armanda, even if she were a thief, is human! But that girl ... There isn't anyone to feel sorry for in this case, Alberto! I'm the one who's the victim ... Even when Joana isn't in the house, I feel on edge. It sounds crazy, but it's as if she were watching me ... reading my thoughts ... Sometimes I'll be laughing and I stop short, cold. Soon, in my own house, my own home, where I raised my daughter, I'll have to apologize to that girl for goodness-knows-what ... She's a viper. She's a cold viper, Alberto, there's no love or gratitude in her. There's no point liking her, no point doing the right thing by her. I think she's capable of killing someone ..."

"Don't say that!" exclaimed the uncle in shock. "If Joana's father were anyone else, he'd roll over in his grave now!"

"Forgive me, I lose my head, she's the one who drives me to speak such heresies ... She's a strange creature, Alberto, with neither friends nor God – may He forgive me!"

Joana's hands moved of their own accord. She watched them vaguely curious and promptly forgot them. The ceiling was white, the ceiling was white. Even her shoulders, which she had always considered so far from herself, palpitated alive, tremulous. Who was she? The viper, Yes, yes, where should she flee? She didn't feel weak, but on the contrary gripped by an uncommon ardor, mixed with a certain happiness, dark and violent. I am suffering, she thought suddenly and surprised herself. I am suffering, a separate awareness told her. And suddenly this other being loomed big and took the place of the one who was suffering. Nothing happened if she kept waiting for what was going to happen … Events could be halted and she could knock about empty like the seconds on the clock. She remained hollow for a few moments, watching herself closely, scrutinizing the return of pain. No, she didn't want it! And as if to stop herself, full of fire, she slapped her own face.

She fled once more to her teacher, who still didn't know she was a viper …

The teacher let her in again, miraculously. And miraculously he penetrated Joana's shadowy world and moved about in it a little, delicately.

"It's not being worth more to others, as regards the ideal human being. It's being worth more inside yourself. Do you understand, Joana?"

"Yes, yes …"

He talked all afternoon.

"Animal life boils down to this pursuit of pleasure after all. Human life is more complex: it boils down to the pursuit of pleasure, to fear of it, and above all to the dissatisfaction of the time in between. What I'm saying is a little simplistic, but it doesn't matter for now. Do you understand? All yearning is pursuit of pleasure. All remorse, pity, benevolence, is fear of it. All despair and seeking alternative routes are dissatisfaction. There you have it in a nutshell, if you wish. Do you understand?"

"Yes."

"Those who deny themselves pleasure, who act like monks, in any sense, it's because they have an enormous capacity for pleasure, a dangerous capacity—hence even greater fear. Only he who is afraid of shooting everyone keeps his guns under lock and key."

"Yes …"

"I said: those who deny themselves … Because there are the … the plans, those made of soil which will never flourish without fertilizer."

"Me?"

"You? No, for heaven's sake … You're one of the ones that would kill to flourish."

She continued listening to him and it was as if her aunt and uncle had never existed, as if the teacher and her were isolated inside the afternoon, inside understanding.

"No, I really don't know what advice I'd give you," said the teacher. "Tell me first of all: what is good and what is bad?"

"I don't know …"

"'I don't know' isn't an answer. Learn to find everything that exists within you."

"Good is living …" she stammered. "Bad is …"

"Is …?"

"Bad is not living …"

"Dying?" he asked.

"No, no …" she groaned.

"What, then? Say it."

"Bad is not living, that's all. Dying is something else. Dying is different to good and bad."

"Yes," he said without understanding. "Anyhow. Tell me now, for example: who is the greatest man alive, in your opinion?"

She thought and thought and didn't answer.

"What is the thing you most like?" he tried.

Joana's face brightened up, she got ready to speak and suddenly discovered that she didn't know what to say."

"I don't know, I don't know," she said in despair.

"But how not? Why then were you almost laughing with pleasure?" said her teacher, surprised.

"I don't know ..."

He gave her a severe look.

"It's alright that you don't know who the greatest man alive is even though you know lots of them. But what bothers me is that you don't know what you feel."

She looked at him in distress.

"Look, the thing I most like in the world ... I feel inside me, kind of opening ... I can almost, almost say what it is but I can't ..."

"Try to explain," he said with furrowed eyebrows.

"It's like a thing that's going to be ... It's like ..."

"It's like...?" he leaned forward, demanding serious.

"It's like a desire to breathe a lot, but also fear ... I don't know ... I don't know, it almost hurts. It's everything ... It's everything."

"Everything ...?" asked the teacher with a puzzled look.

She nodded, choked up, mysterious, intense: "everything ..." He continued to study her for a moment, her little face troubled and powerful.

"Fine."

He seemed satisfied but she didn't know why, since she hadn't actually said anything about "it." But if he said "it's fine," she thought ardently with her soul smitten, if he said "it's fine," it was true.

"Who is the person you most admire? besides me, besides me," he added. If you don't help me, I can't get to know you, I won't be able to guide you."

"I don't know," said Joana, wringing her hands under the table.

"Why didn't you cite one of the great men that are out there? You know at least a dozen of them. You are excessively sincere, excessively," he said with displeasure.

"I don't know ..."

"Fine, it doesn't matter," he said more serenely. "Never suffer because you don't have an opinion on this or that topic. Never suffer because you are not something or because you are. At any rate I imagine you'd only accept this advice. And get used to it: what you felt—about what you most like in the world—may only have been at the expense of not having a precise opinion about great men. You'll have to give up a lot in order to have others." He paused. "Does that bother you?"

Joana thought for a moment, her dark head tilted, eyes open and broad.

"But if you have the highest thing," she said slowly, "don't you already have the things under it so to speak?"

The teacher shook his head.

"No," he said, "no. Not always. Sometimes one has the highest thing and at the end of their life they feel as if ..." – he glanced sideways at her – "they feel as if they're dying a virgin. You see, it may not be a question of things being higher and lower. Different in nature. Do you understand?"

Yes, she was comprehending his words, everything they encompassed. But nevertheless it felt like they had a false door, disguised, through which their true meaning could be found.

"That they're more than what you said, sir," Joana finished his explanation.

In a sudden movement, before interpreting himself, the teacher held out his hand out over the table. Joana shivered with pleasure, gave him hers, blushing.

"What?" she said softly. And she loved that man as if she were a fragile grass and the wind buffeted, flogged her.

He didn't answer, but his eyes were strong and contained pity. "What?" she asked, suddenly frightened:

"What's going to happen to me?"

"I don't know," he answered after a short silence. "Maybe you'll be happy at some point, I don't understand, a happiness that few people will envy. I don't even know if it could be called happiness. You might never find anyone else who feels with you, like …"

The teacher's wife came into the room, tall, almost beautiful with her short, sleek, coppery hair. And above all her tall, serene thighs moving blindly, but full of frightening self-assuredness. What was the teacher about to say, thought Joana, before "she" came in? 'Anyone else who feels with you … like me?' Ah that woman. She glanced at her fugitively, lowered her rage-filled eyes. The teacher was distant again, his hand withdrawn, lips downturned, indifferent as if Joana was nothing but his "little friend," as his wife put it.

The wife walked over, placed her long, white, wax-like, but strangely attractive hand on her husband's shoulder. And Joana saw, full of a pain that made it hard for her to swallow her saliva, the beautiful contrast between the two beings. His hair still black, his body enormous like that of an animal larger than man.

"Would you like your dinner now?" asked his wife.

He was playing with a pencil between his fingers.

"Yes, I'm going out earlier."

The wife smiled at Joana and left slowly.

Still insecure, she thought that once again that creature's passage through the room made it clear that her teacher was a man and Joana wasn't even a "young lady" yet. Would he also notice, dear God, would he at least also notice how hateful that white woman was, how well she knew how to destroy any previous conversation?

"Are you teaching tonight, sir?" she asked hesitantly just to keep the conversation going. And she went red as she uttered the words, so white, so out of line … Not in the tone of voice his wife had used when she asked, beautiful and composed: would you like an early dinner?

"Yes, I am," he replied and shuffled the papers on the table.

Joana got up to leave and suddenly, before she was even aware of her own gesture, sat down again. She slumped over the table and burst into tears hiding her eyes. Around her was silence and she could hear the slow, muffled footsteps of someone in the house. A long minute went past until she felt on her head a light, soft weight, the hand. His hand. She heard the hollow sound of her heart, stopped breathing. She focused her entire self on her own hair which was now living above all, gigantic, nervous, thick under those strange, eager fingers. Another hand lifted her chin and she allowed herself to be examined submissive and trembling.

"What's up?" he asked smiling. "Our conversation?"

Unable to speak, she shook her head.

"What, then?" he insisted in a firm voice.

"It's just that I'm ugly," she answered obediently, her voice stuck in her throat.

He was taken aback. He opened his eyes wider, piercing her in surprise.

"Now," he tried to laugh after a moment, "I'd almost forgotten I was talking to a little girl … Who said you're ugly?" he said, laughing again. "Stand up."

She stood, her heart tight, aware that her knees were grayish and opaque as always.

"Still a little shapeless, it is true, but it'll all get better, don't you worry," he said.

She stared at him from inside her last tears. How to explain to him? She didn't want to be consoled, he hadn't understood … The teacher met her stare with raised eyebrows. What? What? he wondered with displeasure.

She held her breath.

"I can wait."

The teacher didn't breathe for a few seconds either. He asked, his voice the same, suddenly cold:

"Wait for what?"

"Until I become pretty. Pretty like 'her.'"

It was his own fault, was his first thought, like a slap in the face. It was his fault for having leaned too close to Joana, for having sought, yes, sought (don't deny it, don't deny it), thinking he'd get away with it, her promise of youth, that fragile, ardent stalk. And before he could restrain his thought (his hands clenched under the table), it came merciless: the selfishness and brute hunger of the old age that was approaching. Oh, how he hated himself for having thought about that. Was "she," his wife, prettier? The "other one" was too. And "tonight's one" too. But who had that imprecision in her body, the nervous legs, breasts yet to bud (the miracle: yet to be born, he thought dizzily, his vision obscured), who was like clear, fresh water? The hunger of the old age that was approaching. He drew back terrified, furious, cowardly.

His wife came in again. She had changed for the evening, her body strong and limited now behind blue fabric. Her husband took a long look at her, his expression undefined, gaping somewhat. She bore his gaze, a half smile behind her face, serious, enigmatic. Joana shrank, grew small and dark before that radiant skin. She felt the shame of the previous scene wash over her and belittle her ridiculously.

"I'll be going," she said.

The wife—or was she imagining it?—the wife looked her straight in the eye, understanding, understanding! And then she raised her head, her eyes clear and calm in her victory, perhaps with a little congeniality.

"When will you be back Joana? You need to come debate with your teacher more often ..."

With your teacher, she said playing with intimacy, and she was white and smooth. Not miserable and not knowing anything, not abandoned, not dirty-kneed like Joana, like Joana! Joana got up and she knew that her skirt was short, that her blouse was clinging to her minuscule, hesitant bust. Flee, run to the beach, lie face-down in the sand, hide her face, listen to the sound of the sea.

She shook the woman's soft hand, shook his large one, bigger than a man's.

"Don't you want to take the book?"

Joana turned and saw him. She saw his look. Ah, the discovery shone inside her, a look like a handshake, a look that knew she longed for the beach. But why so weak, so cheerless? What had happened after all? Just a few hours earlier people were calling her a viper, the teacher was dashing off, his wife waiting ... What was going on? Everything was receding ... And suddenly the setting stood out in her awareness with a scream, loomed up in all its detail submerging the people in a big wave ... Her very feet were floating. The room where she had spent so many afternoons glittered in the crescendo of an orchestra, silently, avenging itself for her distraction. All at once Joana discovered the unsuspecting potency of that quiet room. It was strange, silent, absent as if no one had ever set foot in it, as if it were a reminiscence. Things had remained hidden until now and were closing in on Joana, surrounding her, glowing in the half darkness of dusk. Perplexed, she saw the nude statue atop the glinting crystal cabinet, with softly tapering lines as if at the end of a movement. The silence of the unmoving, elegant chairs spoke to her brain, emptied it slowly … She heard hurried footsteps outside, saw the big, serious woman looking at her and the strong, curved-backed man too. What did they expect of her? she wondered with a start. She felt the book's hard cover between her fingers, far far away as if an abyss separated her from her own hands. What then? Why did every living thing have something to tell her? Why, why? And what did they require, always draining her? Giddiness, swift as a whirlpool, gripped her head, made her knees buckle. She had been standing in front of them for a few minutes, speechless, feeling the house, but why weren't people entirely surprised by her behavior which to them was inexplicable? Ah, one could expect anything from her, the viper, even things that seemed strange, the viper, oh the pain, happiness hurting. The two of them stood out from the shadows, standing in front of her and only in the teacher's gaze was there a little surprise.

"I felt dizzy," she told them in a low voice and the crystal cabinet continued shining like a saint.

She had barely spoken, her sight still obscured, Joana sensed an almost imperceptible movement in the teacher's wife. They gazed at one another and a hint of something mean, avid and humiliated in the woman made Joana start to understand, dumfounded … It was her second dizzy spell that day! Yes, it was her second dizzy spell that day! Like a bugle … She stared at them intensely. I'm leaving this house, she cried agitated. And the room closed in more and more, from one moment to the next she would awaken fury in the man and his wife! Like rain pouring down, like rain pouring down …

In the sand her feet sunk down and rose up again heavy. It was already night, the sea was rolling dark, nervous, the waves were chomping at one another on the beach. The wind had nested in her hair, making her short fringe flap about like mad. Joana no longer felt giddy, now a brute arm weighed on her chest, a good weight. Something will come soon, she thought quickly. It was her second dizzy spell in one day! That morning, as she got out of bed, and now … I am more and more alive, she understood vaguely. She began to run. She was suddenly freer, angrier at everything, she felt triumphantly. It wasn't anger, however, but love. Love so strong that its passion was only curbed by the strength of hatred. Now I am a viper alone. She remembered that she had really severed ties with her teacher, that after that conversation she could never go back … She felt him far away, in the place that she already remembered with shock and without familiarity. Alone …

Her aunt and uncle were already at the table. But to which of them would she say: I am stronger and stronger, I am growing up, I am almost a woman? Not to them, not to anyone. Because I also won't be able to ask anyone: tell me, how do things work? and hear: I don't know either, as her teacher had answered her. Her teacher reappeared in front of her as he had at the last moment, leaning toward her, startled or fierce, she wasn't sure, but retreating, yes, retreating. His answer, she felt, didn't matter so much. What counted was that her question had been accepted, it could exist. Her aunt would reply, surprised: what things? And if she ever came to understand, she would no doubt say: they work like this, this and that. Now who would Joana talk to about things that existed as naturally as one talked of other things, those that just were?

Things that exist, others that just are … She surprised herself with the new, unexpected thought, which would live from then on like flowers on the grave. Which would live, which would live, other thoughts would be born and live and she herself was more alive. Happiness pierced her heart, ferocious, lit her body. She squeezed the glass between her fingers, drank water with her eyes closed as if it was wine, bloody and glorious wine, the blood of God. Yes, she would explain to neither of them that everything was slowly changing … That she had put away her smile like one who has finally turned off the lamp and decided to go to bed. Now no living thing was allowed in her inner self, merging into it. The way she related to people was becoming increasingly different to the way she related to herself. The sweetness of childhood was disappearing in a few remaining features, a spring's outward flow was stanching and what she offered strangers' footsteps was colorless, dry sand. But she walked forward, always forward as one walks on the beach, the wind caressing her face, blowing her hair back.

How could she share it with them: it was her second dizzy spell in a single day? even if she was burning to confide her secret to someone. Because no one else in her life, no one else perhaps, would say to her, as her teacher had: you live and you die. They all forgot, they all only knew how to play. She looked at them. Her aunt played with a house, a cook, a husband, a married daughter, visitors. Her uncle played with money, with work, with a farm, with games of chess, with newspapers. Joana tried to analyze them, feeling that in this manner she would destroy them. Yes, they were fond of each another in a faraway, old way. From time to time, busy with their toys, they would glance at one another restlessly, as if to make sure they still existed. Then they resumed their lukewarm distance that was occasionally reduced by a cold or a birthday. They no doubt slept together thought Joana without pleasure in her malice.

Her aunt handed her the bread plate in silence. Her uncle didn't take his eyes off the plate.

Food was one of the great concerns of the household, continued Joana. At mealtimes, arms leaning heavily on the table, her uncle fed himself puffing slightly, because he had heart problems, and as he chewed, some forgotten crumbs around his mouth, he would stare off blankly at a fixed point, his attention focused on the inner sensations that the food produced in him. Her aunt crossed her feet under her chair, and, with furrowed eyebrows, ate with a curiosity that was renewed with each forkful, her face rejuvenated and mobile. But why didn't they relax in their chairs today? Why were they taking such care not to clink their cutlery, as if someone were dead or sleeping? It's me, figured Joana.

Around the dark table, in the light weakened by the chandelier's dirty fringes, silence had also taken a seat that night. At times Joana stopped to listen to the sound of the two mouths chewing and the light, nervous ticking of the clock. Then the aunt raised her eyes and frozen with her fork in hand, waited anxiously and humbly. Joana looked away, victorious, lowered her head in a profound happiness that inexplicably came mixed with a painful knot in her throat, an inability to sob.

"Didn't Armanda come?" Joana's voice quickened the ticking of the clock, giving rise to a sudden, rapid movement at the table.

Her aunt and uncle glanced at one another furtively. Joana sighed loudly: so they were afraid of her, were they?

"Armanda's husband isn't on call today. That's why she didn't

come for dinner," her aunt finally replied. And suddenly, satisfied, she resumed eating. Her uncle chewed faster. Silence
returned without dissolving the faraway murmur of the sea.
They didn't have the courage, then.

"When do I leave for boarding school?" asked Joana.

The soup terrine slipped from her aunt's hands, the dark,
cynical broth spreading quickly across the table. Her uncle
abandoned his cutlery on his plate, his face distressed.

"How do you know that …" he stammered, confused …

She had listened at the door …

The drenched tablecloth steamed sweetly like the remains
of a fire. Unmoving and fascinated as if faced with something
irremediable, the aunt stared at the spilt soup that was quickly
cooling.

The water blind and deaf but cheerfully not-mute glinting and
bubbling as it meets the bright enamel of the bathtub. The
room stuffy with warm vapors, the steamed up mirrors, the
reflection of the already naked body of a young woman in the
wet tiles on the walls.

The girl laughs gently out of bodily happiness. Her smooth,
slender legs, her small breasts poke out of the water. She barely
knows herself, she hasn't finished growing, having merely
emerged from childhood. She stretches out a leg, looks at her
foot from afar, moves it tenderly, slowly like a fragile wing. She
raises her arms up over her head, toward the ceiling lost in
the penumbra, eyes closed, without a single feeling, just movement. Her body lengthens, stretches, glistens wet in the half
darkness—it is a tense, tremulous line. When she drops her
arms again she condenses, white and secure. She laughs quietly, moves her long neck from one side to the other, leans her

head back—the grass is always fresh, someone is going to kiss her, soft little rabbits huddle together with their eyes closed.— She laughs again, in light murmurs like those of the water. She strokes her waist, her hips, her life.

She sinks into the tub as if it were the sea. A warm world closes over her silently, quietly. Little bubbles slide softly until they extinguish themselves against the enamel. The young woman feels the water weighing on her body, stops for an instant as if someone has softly tapped her shoulder. Tuned in to what she is feeling, the soft invasion of the tide. What happened? She becomes a serious being, with wide, deep pupils. She barely breathes. What happened? The mute, open eyes of things continue sparkling between vapors. Over the same body that sensed happiness there is water—water. No, no ... Why? Beings born in the world like water. She squirms, tries to get away. "Everything," she says slowly as if surrendering something, scrutinizing herself without understanding herself. Everything. And this word is peace, serious and incomprehensible as a ritual. Water covers her body. But what happened? She murmurs in a low voice, utters warm, molten syllables.

The bathroom is indecisive, almost dead. Objects and walls have given way, softening and diluting themselves in tendrils of steam. The water cools slightly on her skin and she shivers in fear and discomfort.

When she emerges from the tub she is a stranger who doesn't know what to feel. There is nothing around her and she recognizes nothing. Light and sad, she moves slowly, unhurried for a long time. Cold runs its icy feet down her back but she doesn't want to play, she draws in her wounded, unhappy torso. She dries herself off without love, humiliated and poor, wraps herself in a robe as if in lukewarm arms. Closed off inside herself, not wanting to look, ah, not wanting to look, she slides down the corridor—the long red and dark and discreet throat through which she will sink into the essence, into the everything. Everything, everything, she repeats mysteriously. She closes the bedroom windows—see not, hear not, feel not. In her silent bed, floating in the darkness, she curls up as if in the lost womb and forgets. Everything is vague, light and silent.

Behind her the boarding school dormitory beds stood in a straight line. And in front of her the window opened onto the night.

I have discovered a miracle above the rain, thought Joana. A miracle split into chunky, serious, twinkling stars, like a stationary warning: like a lighthouse. What are they trying to say? In them I sense the secret, the twinkling is the impassive mystery I hear flowing inside me, crying in broad, desperate, romantic notes. Dear God, at least allow me to communicate with them, satisfy my desire to kiss them. To feel their light on my lips, feel it glow inside my body, leaving it sparkling and transparent, cool and moist like the minutes before dawn. Why do these strange thirsts grip me? The rain and the stars, this cold, dense mixture woke me up, opened the doors of my green, dark wood, of my wood that smells of an abyss where water flows. And made it one with the night. Here, by the window, the air is calmer. Stars, stars, I pray. The word splinters between my teeth into fragile shards. Because the rain does not fall inside me, I want to be a star. Purify me a little and I will have the mass of those beings that take refuge behind the rain. At this moment my inspiration hurts all over my body. An instant more and it will need to be more than inspiration. And instead of this asphyxiating happiness, like too much air, I will clearly feel the impotence of having more than inspiration, of going beyond it, of possessing the thing itself—and really being a star. Where madness, madness leads. But it is true. What does it matter that I still appear to be in the dormitory at this moment, the other girls dead to the world, bodies unmoving on their beds? What does it matter what really is? I am in fact kneeling, naked as an animal, next to my bed, my soul despairing as only the body of a virgin can despair. The bed slowly disappears, the walls of the room recede, tumble down in defeat. And I am in the world as free and slender as a deer on the plain. I get up as soft as a breath of air, raise my sleepy flower head, my feet light, I cross fields beyond the earth, world, time, God. I dive under and then emerge, as if from clouds, from lands still not possible, ah still not possible. From those that I still don't even know how to imagine, but which will germinate. I walk, glide, on and on … Always, unstopping, diverting my weary longing to reach an end.—Where have I ever seen a moon high in the sky, white and silent? Livid garments fluttering in the wind. The pole without a flag, upright and mute erected in space … Everything waiting for midnight …—I am fooling myself, I need to return. I don't feel madness in my wish to bite stars, but the earth still exists. And because the first truth is in the earth and the body. If the twinkling of the stars pains me, if this distant communication is possible, it is because something almost like a star quivers within me. Here I am back at the body. Return to my body. When I surprise myself in the depths of the mirror I get a fright. I can hardly believe that I have limits, that I am cut out and defined. I feel scattered in the air, thinking inside other beings, living in things beyond myself. When I surprise myself at the mirror I am not frightened because I think I am ugly or beautiful. It is because I discover I am of a different nature. After not having seen myself for a while I almost forget I am human, I forget my past and I am as free from end and awareness as something merely alive. I am also surprised, eyes open at the pale mirror, that there are so many things in me besides what I know, so many things always silent. Why unspeaking? Do these curves beneath my blouse live with impunity? Why unspeaking? My mouth, somewhat childish, so certain of its destiny, is the same as itself despite my utter distraction. At times, following my discovery comes love for myself, a steady gaze in the mirror, an understanding smile for those who stare at me. A period of interrogating my body, of gluttony, of sleep, of long walks in the open air. Until a phrase, a look—like the mirror—reminds me surprised of other secrets, those that make me limitless. Fascinated I plunge my body down to the bottom of the well, silence all of its springs and sleepwalking take another path.— Analyze instant by instant, perceive the nucleus of each thing made of time or space. Own each moment, connect my awareness to them, like tiny filaments almost imperceptible but strong. Is this life? Even so it would give me the slip. Another way to capture it would be to live. But dreams are more complete than reality, which drowns me in the unconscious. What matters then: to live or to know you are living?—Very pure words, droplets of crystal. I feel the shining, moist form thrashing about inside me. But where is what I want to say, where is what I should say? Inspire me, I have almost everything; I have the outline waiting for the essence; is that it?—What should someone who doesn't know what to do with herself do? Use herself as body and soul to make the most of body and soul? Or make her strength into an outside force? Or wait for the solution, like a consequence, to be born of herself? I can't tell still inside the form. Everything I possess is very deep within me. One day, after speaking at last, will I still have something to live on? Or will everything I say fall short of or beyond life?—I try to push away everything that is a life form. I try to isolate myself in order to find life in itself. However I have relied too much on the game that distracts and consoles and when I pull away from it, I find myself brusquely forsaken. The minute I close the door behind me, I let go of things instantly. Everything that was distances itself from me, diving deafly into my faraway waters. I hear it, the fall. Happy and flat I wait for myself, I wait for myself to slowly rise up and truly appear before my eyes. Instead of obtaining myself by fleeing, I find myself forsaken, alone, tossed into a dimensionless cubicle, where light and shadow are quiet ghosts. In my interior I find the silence I seek. But in it I become so lost from any memory of a human being and of myself, that I make this impression into the certainty of physical solitude. If I were to scream—already without lucidity I imagine—my voice would receive the same, indifferent echo of the walls of the earth. Without experiencing things I won't find life, will I? But, even so, in the white, unlimited solitude where I fall, I am still stuck between closed mountains. Stuck, stuck. Where is the imagination? I walk on invisible tracks. Captivity, freedom. These are the words that occur to me. However they are not the true, only, irreplaceable ones, I feel. Freedom isn't enough. What I desire doesn't have a name yet.—I am thus a toy that is wound up and which when done will not find its own, deeper life. Try to calmly admit that I may only find it if I look for it in the small springs. Otherwise I will die of thirst. Maybe I wasn't made for pure, wide waters, but for the small ones that are easy to get to. And maybe my desire for another spring, this keenness that gives my face the look of one who hunts to eat, maybe this keenness is just an idea—and nothing more. However—the rare instants I sometimes come by of sufficiency, of blind life, of happiness as intense and serene as organ music—don't these instants prove that I am capable of fulfilling my quest and that this is the longing of my entire being and not just an idea? Besides which, the idea is the truth! I cry. These instants are rare. When yesterday, in class, I suddenly thought, almost without antecedents, almost without connection to things: movement explains form. The clear notion of perfection, the sudden freedom I felt ... That day, on my uncle's farm, when I fell in the river. Before I was closed, opaque. But, when I stood up, it was as if I had been born of the water. I came out wet, clothes clinging to my skin, hair shining, down. Something or other stirred in me and it was no doubt just my body. But in a sweet miracle everything had become transparent and it was no doubt my soul too. At this instant I was truly immersed in my interior and there was silence. Except that my silence, I understood, was part of the silence of the countryside. And I didn't feel forsaken. The horse from which I had fallen was waiting for me by the river. I mounted it and flew down slopes that shadows had already invaded and cooled. I reined it in, ran my hand along the animal's warm, throbbing neck. I continued at a slow pace, listening to the happiness inside me, as high and pure as a summer sky. I stroked my arms, where water still dripped. I felt the horse alive near me, an extension of my body. Both of us breathed palpitating and new. A softly somber color had settled on the fields warm from the last sunlight and the light breeze flew slowly. I must not forget, I thought, that I have been happy, that I am being happier than one can be. But I forgot, I've always forgotten.

I was sitting in the Cathedral, in distracted, vague waiting. I was breathing oppressed the cold, purple perfume of the statues. And, suddenly, before I could understand what was going on, like a cataclysm, the invisible organ unfurled in full, tremulous, pure sounds. Without melody, almost without music, almost vibration alone. The church's long walls and high vaults received the notes and returned them sonorous, nude and intense. They pierced me, crisscrossed inside me, filled my nerves with tremors, my brain with sounds. I wasn't thinking thoughts, but music. Numbly, under the weight of the canticle, I slid from the pew and knelt without praying, annihilated. The organ fell silent with the same suddenness with which it had begun, like a flash of inspiration. I kept breathing quietly, my body still vibrating to the last sounds remaining in the air in a warm, translucent drone. And the moment was so perfect that I neither feared nor gave thanks for anything and I was not drawn into the idea of God. I want to die now, cried something inside me freed, more than suffering. Any instant following that one would be lower and emptier. I wanted to rise and only death like an end, would give me the peak without the decline. People were getting up round me, moving about. I stood, walked to the exit, fragile and pale.

The Woman with the Voice and Joana

JOANA DIDN'T PAY HER TOO MUCH ATTENTION UNTIL she heard her voice. Its low, curved tone, without vibrations, roused her. She stared at the woman inquisitively. She must have experienced something that Joana had yet to go through. She didn't understand that intonation, so far from life, so far from days …

Joana remembered how once, a few months after she was married, she had turned to her husband to ask him something. They were out. And before she'd even finished her sentence, to Otávio's surprise, she had stopped — brow furrowed, gaze amused. Ah — she had realized — she'd just repeated one of the voices she'd heard so often when she was single, always vaguely perplexed. The voice of a young woman beside her man. As her own had rung out just then to Otávio: sharp, empty, soaring upwards, with identical, clear notes. Something unfinished, ecstatic, somewhat satiated. Trying to scream … Bright days, clear and dry, sexless voice and days, choir boys in an outdoor mass. And something lost, heading for mild despair … That newlywed timbre had a history, a fragile history that went unnoticed by the owner of the voice, but not by the owner of this one.

From that day on, Joana felt voices. She understood them or didn't understand them. No doubt at the end of her life, for each timbre heard a wave of her own reminiscences would surface to memory, she'd say: how many voices I've had ...

She leaned towards the woman. She had arrived at her while looking for a house to live in and she was thankful she hadn't gone with her husband because, on her own, she was freer to observe. And there, yes, there was something she hadn't expected, a pause. But the woman didn't even look at her. Thinking through Otávio's head, Joana figured he'd merely find her vulgar, with that large, pale, calm nose. The gal was explaining the conveniences and inconveniences of the house for rent, all the while running her eyes over the ground, the window, the landscape, without impatience, without interest. Her clean body, dark hair. Big, strong. And her voice, an earthy voice. Without bumping into any object, soft and faraway as if it had undertaken long journeys under the ground before reaching her throat.

"Married?" asked Joana, hovering over her.

"Widowed, with one son." And she continued distilling her song about rentals in the region.

"No, I don't think the house is right. It's too big for a couple," said Joana in a hurry, a little gruffly. "But," she said sweetening her words, concealing her eagerness, "could I visit you now and then for a chat?"

The woman wasn't surprised. She smoothed a hand over her waist thickened by motherhood and by the slowness of movements:

"I don't think it'll be possible ... I'm going to visit my son tomorrow. He's married. I'm going away ..."

She smiled without cheer, without emotion. Just: I'm going

away. What was that woman interested in? wondered Joana. Might she have a lover ...

"Do you live alone, ma'am?" she asked her.

"My youngest sister became a sister of charity. I live with the other one."

"Isn't it sad living without a man in the house?" continued Joana.

"Do you think?" replied the woman.

"I'm asking if you think so, ma'am, not me. I'm married," she added, trying to give the conversation an intimate tone.

"Nah, I don't think it's sad." And she smiled colorlessly. "Well, if you'll excuse me I'll be on my way then, since you're not interested in the house. I need to wash some clothes before I take some air at the window."

Joana went on her way humiliated. Definitely feebleminded ... But what about the voice? She was unable to shake it for the rest of the afternoon. Her imagination raced to find the woman's smile, her broad, quiet body. She had no history, Joana slowly realized. Because if things happened to her, they were not her and didn't mix with her true existence. The main thing—including past, present and future—was that she was alive. This was the backdrop of the narrative. At times this backdrop seemed faded, eyes closed, almost inexistent. But all it took was a tiny pause, a short silence, for it to loom up in the foreground, eyes open, a light, constant burbling like that of water between stones. Why describe more than that? Things outside of her had no doubt happened to her. She had been disillusioned, had the odd bout of pneumonia. Things happened to her. But they only intensified or weakened the burbling at her center. At the end of the day, why talk about facts and details if none of them dominated her? And if she was just the life that coursed through her body without ceasing?

Her interrogations never went restlessly looking for answers—Joana continued to realize. They were born dead, smiling, piling up without desire or hope. She didn't attempt any movement outside of herself.

Many years of her existence she had spent at the window, watching the things that passed and those that stayed still. But in fact she didn't see so much as hear the life inside her. She was fascinated by its noise—like the breathing of a tender child, by its sweet glow—like a newly-born plant. She still hadn't tired of existing and she was enough so much so that at times, enormously happy, she felt sadness cover her like the shadow of a blanket, leaving her as cool and silent as nightfall. She expected nothing. She was in herself, the end itself.

One day she split into two, grew restless, started going out to look for herself. She went to places where men and women met. Everyone said: fortunately she has woken up, life is short, one needs to make the most of it, she used to be lackluster, now she is somebody. No one knew she was being so unhappy that she needed to go looking for life. That was when she picked a man, loved him and love came to thicken her blood and the mystery. She gave birth to a son, her husband died after impregnating her. She carried on and developed very well. She gathered up all of her pieces and didn't seek other people any more. Once more she found the window where she'd go sit in her own company. And now, more than ever, there had never been a happier or more complete thing or being. Even though many looked down on her, believing her weak. For her spirit was so strong that she had never stopped eating well at lunch and dinner, without an excess of pleasure incidentally. Nothing that anyone said mattered to her, neither did events, and everything slid over her and was lost in waters other than her inner ones.

One day, after living through many identical ones without boredom, she found herself different to herself. She was tired. She paced to and fro. She herself didn't know what she wanted. She started singing quietly, her mouth closed. Then she grew tired and started thinking about things. But she wasn't able to wholly. Inside her something was trying to stop. She waited and nothing came from her to her. She slowly saddened with a sadness that was insufficient and thus doubly sad. She kept pacing for several days and her footsteps sounded like dead leaves falling to the ground. She was lined with gray on the inside and saw nothing in herself except a reflection, like white drops dripping, a reflection of her old rhythm, now slow and thick. Then she knew that she was drained and for the first time suffered because she really had split into two, each part facing the other, watching her, wishing for things that the other could no longer give. In truth she had always been two, the one that had a slight idea that she was and the one that actually was, profoundly. It was just that until then the two of them had worked together and couldn't be told apart. Now the one that knew she was worked on her own, which meant that the woman was being unhappy and intelligent. She tried in a last-ditch effort to invent something, a thought, to distract herself. Useless. All she knew how to do was live.

Until the absence of herself ended up making her fall into the night and pacified, darkened and cool, she began to die. Then she died gently, as if she were a ghost. Nothing else is known because she died. One can only guess that in the end she was also being as happy as a thing or creature can be. Because she had been born for the essential, to live or to die. And everything in between was suffering for her. Her existence was so complete and so connected to the truth that when it came time to give in and die she probably thought, if indeed she was in the habit of thinking: I never was. It is also not known what became of her. Such a fine life must have been followed by a fine death too. She is no doubt grains of earth today. She gazes up at the sky, the whole time. Sometimes it rains and she becomes full and round in her grains. Then the heat dries her out and any old wind disperses her. She is eternal now.

After a moment of absorption, Joana realized she envied her, that half-dead being who had smiled and spoken to her in an unknown tone of voice. First and foremost, she thought, she understands life because she isn't intelligent enough not to. But what was the point of any reasoning … If you rose to the point of understanding it, without going crazy in the meantime, it wouldn't be possible to preserve the knowledge of it as knowledge but it would be turned into an attitude, an attitude of life, the only way to fully possess and express it. And this attitude wouldn't be all that different to that on which the woman with the voice was based. The courses of action were so poor.

She had a rapid head movement, impatient. She picked up a pencil and on a piece of paper, wrote in intentionally firm writing: "The personality that ignores itself fulfils itself more completely." True or false? But in a way she had avenged herself by casting her cold, intelligent thoughts over that woman swollen with life.

Otávio

"DE PROFUNDIS." JOANA WAITED FOR THE IDEA TO BE-come clearer, for that light, shiny ball that was the germ of a thought to rise up out of the fog. "De profundis." She felt it teeter, almost lose its balance and plunge forever into unknown waters. Or, at times, part the clouds and tremulously grow, almost emerging completely … Then silence.

She closed her eyes, resting at a leisurely pace. When she opened them she got a small shock. And for long, profound seconds she knew that that stretch of life was a mixture of what she had already lived and what she had yet to live, all fused together and eternal. Strange, strange. The orangey 9 o'clock light, that sense of interval, a faraway piano insisting on the high notes, her heart quickly beating against the morning heat and, behind everything, ferocious, menacing, the silence throbbing thick and impalpable. Everything dissipated. The piano stopped insisting on the top notes and after a moment's rest sweetly returned to some middle sounds, in a clear, easy melody. And soon she wouldn't be able to tell if her impression of the morning had been real or just an idea. She stayed alert in order to recognize it … A sudden weariness confused her for a moment. Her nerves abandoned, face relaxed, she felt a light wave of tenderness for herself, of almost thankfulness, though she didn't know why. For a minute it seemed to her that she had already lived and was at the end. And right afterwards, that everything had been blank until now, like an empty space, and that she could hear far off and muffled the din of life approaching, dense, frothy and violent, its tall waves cutting across the sky, drawing nearer, nearer … to submerge her, to submerge her, drown her asphyxiating her …

She went over to the window, stuck her arms out and waited in vain for a little breeze to come caress them. She forgot herself like that for a long time. She kept her ears half closed by contracting her face muscles, her closed eyes barely letting any light through, her head projected forward. Little by little she managed to really isolate herself. This somewhat unconscious state, where she felt like she was deeply immersed in gray, lukewarm air … She stood in front of the mirror and between clenched teeth, eyes stinging with hatred, asked, "What now?"

She couldn't help but notice her own face, tiny and ablaze. She was distracted by it for a moment, forgetting her anger. Precisely always a small thing happened to distract her from the main torrent. She was so vulnerable. Did she hate herself for it? No, she'd hate herself more if she were already a trunk immutable until death, only capable of yielding fruit but not of growing within itself. She wanted even more: to be reborn always, to sever everything that she had learned, that she had seen, and inaugurate herself in new terrain where every tiny act had a meaning, where the air was breathed as if for the first time. She had the feeling that life ran thick and slow inside her, bubbling like a hot sheet of lava. Maybe she loved herself

... And what if she thought distantly, a bugle suddenly cut through that mantle of night with its sharp sound and left the plains free, green and vast ... And then nervous white horses with rebellious neck and leg movements, almost flying, crossed rivers, mountains, valleys ... Thinking of them, she felt the cool air circulate inside herself as if it had come out of a cool, moist, hidden grotto in the middle of the desert.

But she soon returned to herself, in a vertical drop. She examined her arms, her legs. There she was. There she was. But she needed to find a distraction, she thought with harshness and irony. With urgency. For wasn't she going to die? She laughed out loud and glanced at herself quickly in the mirror to see the effect of her laughter on her face. No, it didn't light it up. She looked like a wildcat, her eyes burning over her flaming cheeks, speckled with dark freckles, unkempt brown hair over her eyebrows. She saw dark, triumphant crimson in herself. What was making her glow so much? Boredom ... Yes, in spite of everything there was fire under it, there was fire even when it represented death. Maybe this was the joy of living.

Again she was gripped by restlessness, pure, without reasoning. Ah, maybe I should walk, maybe ... She closed her eyes a moment, allowing herself the birth of a gesture or a sentence without logic. She always did this, trusting that deep down, beneath the lava, there was a desire already headed for an end. At times, when through a special mechanism, the same way one slides into sleep, she closed the doors of her conscience and allowed herself to act or speak, she was surprised—because her perception of the gesture only came to her at the moment of its execution—by her own hands slapping her own face. At times she heard strange, crazy words coming from her own mouth. Even without understanding them, they left her lighter, more liberated. She repeated the experiment, her eyes closed.

And from deep down inside herself, after a moment of silence and abandonment, it rose up, at first pale and hesitant, then stronger and more painful: from the depths I call thee … from the depths I call thee … from the depths I call thee … She remained unmoving for a few more moments, her face expressionless, slack and tired as if she'd had a child. Little by little she was reborn, slowly opened her eyes and returned to the daylight. Fragile, breathing lightly, happy like a convalescent receiving her first breeze.

Then she started to think that in fact she had prayed. Not her. Something more than her, of which she was no longer aware, had prayed. But I didn't mean to pray, she repeated once again weakly. She didn't want to because she knew it would be the remedy. But a remedy like morphine which dulls any kind of pain. Like morphine of which ever-increasing doses are required in order to feel it. No, she still wasn't so worn out that she wanted cowardly to pray instead of discovering pain, suffering it, owning it entirely so she could know all of its mysteries. And even if she did pray … She'd end up in a convent, because for her hunger almost all morphine would be too little. And that would be the final disgrace, the vice. However, along a natural path, if she didn't seek an external god she'd end up deifying herself, exploring her own pain, loving her past, seeking refuge and warmth in her own thoughts, by that time already born aspiring to works of art and then serving as stale food in sterile periods. There was a danger of establishing herself in suffering and organizing herself in it, which would also be a vice and a tranquilizer.

What to do then? What to do to interrupt that path, grant

herself an interval between her and herself, so that she could later find herself again without danger, new and pure?

What to do?

The piano was deliberately attacked in strong, uniform scales. Exercises, she thought. Exercises ... Yes, she discovered amused ... Why not? Why not try to love? Why not try to live?

Pure music developing in a land without men, mused Otávio. Movements as yet without adjectives. As unconscious as the primitive life that pulses in the blind and deaf trees, in the tiny insects that are born, fly, die and are reborn without witnesses. While music whirls around and develops, the dawn, the strong day and the night all live, with a constant note in the symphony, that of transformation. It is music unsupported by things, space or time, the same color as life and death. Life and death in ideas, isolated from pleasure and pain. So far from human qualities that they could blend into the silence. Silence, because this music would be the necessary, the only possible, vibrant projection of matter. And in the same manner because you don't understand matter or perceive it until your senses collide with it, its music wouldn't be heard.

Then what? he thought. Close my eyes and hear my own that oozes along sluggish and cloudy like a muddy river. Cowardice is lukewarm and I resign myself to it, laying down all of the hero's weapons that twenty-seven years of thinking have afforded me. What am I, at this moment? A flat, silent leaf that has fallen to the ground. No gust of air swaying it. Barely breathing so as not to awaken itself. But why, first and foremost why not use proper words and curl up, seek comfort in images? Why call myself a dead leaf when I am just a man with his arms folded?

Once again, in the middle of his useless reasoning, a tiredness came over him, a falling feeling. Pray, pray. Kneel before God and ask. For what? Absolution. Such a wide word, so full of meanings. He wasn't guilty—or was he? of what? he knew he was, but he continued with the thought—he wasn't guilty, but how he wanted to receive absolution. God's broad, fat fingers on his forehead, blessing him as a good father, a father made of earth and world, containing everything, everything, without relinquishing a single particle that could later say to him: yes, but I haven't forgiven you! Then that silent accusation that all things nurtured against him would cease.

What was he thinking after all? How long had he been playing on his own although unmoving? He made some kind of gesture.

Cousin Isabel came in. "Blessed, blessed, blessed," she said her gaze hurried and myopic, anxious to leave. She only dropped that air of a foreigner when she sat at the piano. Otávio shrank back as he had when he was a boy. She then smiled, she was human, she actually lost her piercing air. She took on a flat, easier quality. Sitting at the piano, her lips floury and old, she played Chopin, Chopin, especially all his waltzes.

"My fingers have grown stiff," she'd say proud that she could play by heart. As she spoke, she'd move her head back in a suddenly flirtatious, cabaret-dancer kind of way. Otávio would blush. Prostitute, he'd think, then he'd immediately erase the word with a painful movement. But how dare he? He remembered her face leaning attentively over him, looking after his stomach aches. I detest her for that very reason, he'd think without logic. And it was always too late: the thought preceded him. Prostitute—as if he were beating himself with a whip. Even as he regretted it, however, he sinned again. How many times, as a child, an instant before falling asleep, had he become suddenly aware that cousin Isabel was on the bed, sleepless, perhaps sitting, her gray hair in a braid, her thick nightdress closed like a virgin's. He felt remorse like an acid spreading through his body. But he hated her more and more for not being able to love her.

She was no longer able to move softly from one note to the next as she had in the past, like a faint. One sound would catch on the next, rough, syncopated, and the waltzes erupted weak, jumpy and full of gaps. Sometimes the slow, hollow chimes of the old clock would split the piece into asymmetrical bars. Otávio would wait for the next blow, his heart in his mouth. As if they precipitated all things in a silent, sweetly demented dance. Those beats cutting through the music unrelentingly, always in the same cold, smiling tone, hurled him into himself as if into a vacuum without support. He'd observe his cousin's stiff back, her hands—two dark animals skipping over the piano's yellow keys. She'd turn and tell him, bestowing the phrase out of sheer euphoria, lightly, as if tossing flowers:

"What's up with you? I'm going to play something merrier …"

One of those ballroom waltzes would ensue, naïve and jittery, which he never remembered having heard but which mysteriously latched onto old passages in his memory.

"That one no, cousin, that one no …"

It was too comical. He was afraid. Beg forgiveness for not going into raptures over her music, beg forgiveness for finding her unbearable ever since he was a boy, with that smell of old rags of hers, of musty jewels, when he saw her preparing her "tea to ward off ailments," when she promised to play him something very pretty if he studied hard. He remembered her leaving the house, the light, white powder on her grey skin, the large round neckline revealing her neck where the veins labored, tragic. Her flat-heeled, girly shoes, the umbrella used with terrifying boldness, as a cane. Beg forgiveness for wishing—no, no!—that she would finally die.—He shivered, began to sweat. But it's not my fault! Oh, to leave, to carry out his plan for the book on civil law, to get away from that horrible, repugnantly intimate, human world.

"Here then is "Rustle of Spring …" said cousin Isabel.

Yes, yes. I want the spring … Lord help me. I'm suffocating. The ridiculous spring was even more spring and gaiety.

"This song is like a blue rose," she said half turned towards him with a slightly malicious smile. On her dry, wrinkled face, suddenly a vein of water in the desert, two tiny brilliants quivered from her sagging ears, two tiny wet drops, scintillating. Ah, they were excessively fresh and voluptuous … The old lady had means. But if she wore the dangly earrings it was for a reason he'd never known: she'd bought the stones herself, had them set in earrings, carried them around like two ghosts under her bristly gray hair.

This song is like a blue rose, she had said well aware that only she could understand it. Based on experience he knew he should ask her what she meant and patiently give her the pleasure of answering, as he bit his bottom lip:

"Ah, that's for me to know."

This time however the exciting old game didn't take place. He just avoided looking at her and finding her disappointment. He got up and went to knock on his fiancée's door.

She was sewing by the window. He closed the door, locked it with the key, knelt beside her. He leaned his head against her breast and once again breathed in the warm, sweet perfume of old roses. She continued smiling, absent, almost mysterious, as if listening to the soft rolling of a river within her bosom.

"Otávio, Otávio," she said with her voice sweet, faraway.

None of the inhabitants of that house, not his spinster cousin, not Lídia, not the servants, lived, thought Otávio. Not true, he answered himself back: only he was dead. But he continued: ghosts, ghosts. Their voices distant, no expectations, happiness.

"Lídia," he said, "forgive me."

"But what for?" she asked, discretely alarmed.

"Everything."

Vaguely she thought she should agree and said nothing. Otávio, Otávio. So much easier to talk to other people. If she didn't want him so badly, how hard it would be to bear all that incomprehension on his part. They only understood one another when they kissed, when Otávio leaned his head like that, against her breast. But life was longer, she thought frightened. There would be moments in which she'd look him in the face without her hand being able to reach his. And then—the silence weighing in. He'd always be separated from her and they'd only communicate in the remarkable moments —when there was lots of life and when there was a threat of death. But it wasn't enough, it wasn't enough … Life together was necessary precisely to live the other moments, she thought frightened, reasoning with effort. To Otávio she'd only be able to say the indispensible words, as if he were a god in a hurry. If she rambled on in one of those leisurely, aimless chats, which gave her so much pleasure, she noticed his impatience or his excessively patient, heroic face. Otávio, Otávio … What to do? His approach was a touch of magic, it made her into a being truly alive, every fiber breathing full of blood. Or else he didn't stir her. He put her to sleep as if he'd come simply, quietly, to perfect her.

She knew it was useless to deliberate on her own destiny. She had loved Otávio since the moment he had wanted her, since they were little, under the cheerful gaze of their cousin. And she would always love him. Useless taking other paths, when her steps guided her to only one. Even when he hurt her, she took refuge in him against him. She was so weak. Instead of suffering when she recognized her weakness, she was gladdened: she knew vaguely, without explaining herself, that it was from this that her support for Otávio came. She sensed that he suffered, that he harbored something alive and sick in his soul and that she would only be able to help him by mustering all of the passivity that lay dormant in her being.

Sometimes she rebelled distantly: life is long ... She feared the days, one after another, without surprises, of pure devotion to a man. To a man who would freely use of all of his wife's forces for his own bonfire, in a serene, unconscious sacrifice of everything that wasn't his own personality. It was a false rebellion, an attempt at liberation that came above all with great fear of victory. She'd seek for a few days to take an attitude of independence, which she only achieved with some success in the mornings, when she woke up, when she still hadn't seen him. All it took was his presence, merely sensed, for her entire self to annul itself and wait. At night, alone in her room, she wanted him. All of her nerves, all of her sick muscles. So she resigned herself. Resignation was sweet and fresh. She had been born for it.

Otávio looked at her dark hair, modestly pulled back behind her large, ugly ears. He looked at her thick, firm body, like a tree trunk, her solid, beautiful hands. And, again, like the soft chorus of a song, he repeated: "What connects me to her?" He felt sorry for Lídia, knowing that, even without a motive, even without having met another woman, although she was the only one, he would leave her at some point. Maybe even the very next day. Why not?

"You know?" he said, "I had a dream about you last night."

She opened her eyes, lighting up entirely:

"Really? What?"

"I dreamed that the two of us were strolling through a field full of flowers, that I was picking lilies for you, that you were dressed all in white."

"What a lovely dream …"

"Yes, very lovely …"

"Otávio."

"Yes…?"

"Do you mind if I ask? When are we going to get married? There's nothing stopping us … I need to know because of the linens."

"Is that the only reason?"

She blushed, pleased to be able to say something that made her prettier. She tried awkwardly to act coquettish:

"It's that and … also because I don't want to wait. It's so hard."

"I understand. But I don't know when."

"But why not immediately? You should decide … It's been such a long time since …"

Suddenly Otávio got up and said:

"Do you know it's a lie? That I didn't dream about you?"

She looked at him in alarm, pale.

"You're joking …"

"No, I'm serious. I didn't dream about you."

"Who did you dream about?"

"Nobody. I slept straight through, with no dreams."

She resumed her sewing.

◆

Joana ran her hand over the dog's bloated belly, stroking it with her slender hands. She held back slightly alert.

"She's pregnant," she said.

And there was something in her gaze, in her hands patting the body of the dog that connected her directly to reality laying her bare. As if the two of them formed a single continuous block. There they were, the woman and the dog, alive and naked, with something ferocious in the communion. She speaks with a horrifying precision of terms, thought Otávio uneasily, feeling suddenly useless and effeminate. And it was only the first time he'd seen her.

There was a hard, crystalline quality in her that attracted and repulsed him at the same time, he noticed. Even the way she walked. Without tenderness and pleasure in her own body, but thrusting it like an affront at everyone's eyes, coldly. Otávio watched her move and reflected that not even physically was she the woman he'd like. He preferred small bodies, concluded, without intentions. Or large, like his fiancée's, stationary, silent. Whatever he told them would be enough. Those lines of Joana's, fragile, a sketch, were uncomfortable. They were full of meaning, with open, incandescent eyes. She wasn't pretty, too thin. Even her sensuality must have been be different to his, excessively luminous.

Otávio had sought, from the moment he met her, not to miss any of her details, telling himself: may no feeling of tenderness crystallize in me; I need to see her properly. However, as if she had sensed she was being examined, Joana turned to him at that precise moment, smiling, cold, not very passive. And foolishly he acted, spoke, confused and in a hurry to obey her. Instead of making her reveal herself and thus destroy herself in his power. And despite that air of one who was oblivious to the most ordinary things, like the very first time they had met she had flung him into himself! She had cast him into his own intimacy, coldly forgetting the comfortable little formulas that sustained him and made it easier for him to communicate with people.

Joana told him …

…The old man walked over, his fat body shaking, his skull smooth. He came up to her, lips in a pucker, eyes round, voice weepy. He said, imitating a child's speech:

"I got a boo-boo … It hurts … I took my medicine like a good boy, it's a little better …"

He rolled his eyes back and for a moment his rolls of lard shook, the shine of his moist, saggy lips glistened gently. Leaning a little, Joana saw his empty gums.

"Aren't you going to say you feel sorry for me?"

She gazed at him seriously. He was unfazed:

"Aren't you even going to say 'poor little thing?'"

Seeing him short, backside protruding, big eyes staring, in a large shaky salute was enough to make a person split their sides with laughter and perplexity. She remained silent. Then, slowly, in the same tone:

"Poor thing."

He laughed, considered the game over and turned to the door. Joana followed him with her eyes, leaning a little to reach all of him with her sight, as soon as he moved away from the table. She faced him upright and cold, her eyes open, clear. She glanced at the table, searched a moment, picked up a thick little book. Just as he was placing his hand on the latch, he got it on the back of his neck, with all her strength. He swung around, hand on his head, eyes wide with pain and shock. Joana remained in the same position. Well, she thought, now he's lost that repugnant air. An old man should only suffer. She said in a loud, friendly voice:

"Forgive me. A little lizard there, above the door." Short pause. "I missed."

The old man kept looking at her, not understanding. Then a vague terror gripped him as he stared at that smiling face.

"See you later … It was nothing …" My God! "See you later …"

After the door had closed, the smile stayed on her face a while. She shrugged slightly. She went to the window, her gaze tired and empty:

"Maybe I should listen to music."

"Yes, it's true, I threw the book at him," Joana answered Otávio's question.

He tried to get the upper hand:

"But you didn't tell the old man that!"

"No, I lied."

Otávio studied her, looked in vain for some kind of remorse, some sign of confession.

"Only after I've lived more or better, will I manage to depreciate what is human," Joana sometimes told him. "Human— me. Human—mankind separated into individuals. To forget them because my relationships with them can only be sentimental. If I seek them out, I demand or give them the equivalent of the same old words we always hear, "fraternity," "justice." If they had any real value, it wouldn't be because they are the apex, but the base of a triangle. They'd be the condition rather than the fact itself. Yet they end up occupying all of our mental and emotional space precisely because they are impossible to realize, they are against nature. They are fatal, in spite of everything, in the state of promiscuity in which we live. In this state hatred becomes love, which is really no more than the quest for love, never attained except in theory, as in Christianity.

Oh, spare me, bellowed Otávio. She had wanted to stop but tiredness and the excitement of his presence sharpened her mind and the words poured out unceasing.

"It's hard to depreciate what is human," she went on, "hard to escape this atmosphere of failed revolt (adolescence), of solidarity with others whose efforts have also been impotent. But how good it would be to build something pure, free of false sublimated love, free of the fear of not loving … Fear of not loving, worse than the fear of not being loved …"

Oh, spare me, Joana heard in Otávio's silence. But at the same time she liked to think out loud, to develop a line of reasoning without a plan, just following it. Sometimes, for the sheer pleasure of it, she even invented reflections: if a rock falls, the rock exists, there was a force that caused it to fall, a place from which it fell, a place where it fell, a place through which it fell—I don't think anything has escaped the nature of the fact, except the very mystery of the fact. But now she was also talking because she didn't know how to give herself and especially because she just sensed, without understanding, that Otávio might embrace her and give her peace.

"One night, I'd only just lain down," she told him, "when one of the legs of the bed collapsed throwing me to the ground. After an irate movement, because I wasn't at least sleepy enough to go without comfort, I suddenly thought: why a whole bed and not a broken one? I lay down and was soon asleep …"

She wasn't pretty. Sometimes it was as if her spirit abandoned her and then that which was never discovered through superhuman vigilance (imagined Otávio), revealed itself. On the face that then appeared, the poor, limited features had no beauty of their own. Nothing remained of her former mystery except the color of her skin, cream, somber, fugitive. If the moments of abandonment stretched out and succeeded one another, then with a fright he'd see ugliness, and more than ugliness, a kind of vileness and brutality, something blind and inescapable take over Joana's body as if in a decomposition. Yes, yes, perhaps something released by her fear of not loving then rose to the surface.

"Yes, I know," continued Joana. "The distance that separates emotions from words. I've already thought about that. And the most curious thing is that the moment I try to speak not only do I fail to express what I feel but what I feel slowly becomes what I say. Or at least what makes me act is not, most certainly, what I feel but what I say."

She had talked about the old man, about the dog's pregnancy when he had only just met her and suddenly, frightened, he had felt as one does after a confession, as if he had told that stranger his whole life. What life? That which thrashed about inside him and wasn't anything, he repeated to himself afraid of seeing himself as grandiose and full of responsibilities. — He was nothing, he was nothing and needed thus to do nothing, he repeated to himself, eyes mentally closed. — As if he had told Joana the things he didn't feel except in the dark. And most surprising of all: as if she had listened and laughed afterwards, forgiving (not like God, but like the devil), opening wide doors for him to pass through.

Above all the moment he touched her, he had understood: whatever came to pass between them would be irremediable. Because when he embraced her, he had felt her suddenly come to life in his arms like running water. And seeing her so alive, he had understood crushed and secretly pleased that if she

wanted him he wouldn't be able to do anything about it …
When he finally kissed her he himself had felt suddenly free,
forgiven beyond what he knew of himself, forgiven in what lay
beneath everything he was …

From then on he had no choice. He had fallen vertigi-
nously from Lídia to Joana. Knowing this he helped himself
to love her. It wasn't hard. Once she had been distracted gazing through the window, lips slack, forgetting herself. He had
called her and the soft, abandoned way she had turned her
head and said: what…? had made him fall into himself, plung-
ing into a giddy, dark wave of love. Otávio had then turned his
face away, not wanting to see her.

He could love her, he could take the new, incomprehensible
adventure that she offered him. But he was still clinging to the
first impulse that had thrust him at her. It wasn't as a woman, it
wasn't like that, surrendered, that he wanted her … He needed
her cold and confident. So he could say as he did when he was
a boy, sheltered and almost victorious: it's not my fault …

They'd marry, they'd see one another minute by minute and
may she be worse than he. And strong, to teach him not to be
afraid. Not even the fear of not loving … He wanted her not so
he could make his life with her, but so she could allow him to
live. To live above himself, above his past, above the small vile
acts he had cowardly committed and to which he cowardly remained attached. Otávio thought that by Joana's side he could
continue sinning.

When Otávio had kissed her, he had held her hands, pressing them to her breast, Joana had bitten her lips at first full of
anger because she still didn't know with what thought to dress
that violent sensation, like a scream, which rose up from her
chest until it made her head spin. She looked at him without

seeing him, eyes cloudy, body suffering. They needed to say goodbye. She pulled away brusquely and left without looking back, not missing him.

In her room, already undressed on her bed, she couldn't get to sleep. Her body felt heavy, it existed beyond her like a stranger. She felt it palpitating, on fire. She turned off the light and closed her eyes, tried to escape, to sleep. But she continued scrutinizing herself for many hours, keeping a watch on the blood that dragged itself thick through her veins like a drunken animal. And thinking. As if she hadn't known herself until then. Her slight, slender forms, her delicate adolescent's lines. They opened, breathed suffocated and full to brimming with themselves.

At dawn a sea breeze caressed the bed, waved the curtains. Joana softly relaxed. The coolness of the end of the night caressed her aching body. Tiredness took her slowly and suddenly exhausted she fell into a deep sleep.

She awoke late and cheerful. Each cell, she imagined, had opened florescent. All of her energy miraculously awakened, ready to fight. When she thought about Otávio, she breathed carefully as if the air harmed her. In the days that followed she didn't see him nor did she try to. In fact she avoided him as if his presence were dispensable.

And she was so body that she was pure spirit. She passed through events and hours immaterial, slipping between them with the lightness of an instant. She barely ate and her sleep was as fine as a veil. She'd awaken several times a night, without a start, preparing to smile before thinking. She'd fall asleep again without changing position, just closing her eyes. She looked for herself a lot in the mirror, loving herself without vanity. Her serene skin, vivid lips made her almost timid turn her back on her image, without the strength to sustain her gaze against that woman's, fresh and wet, so mildly clear and self-assured.

Then happiness ceased.

Plenitude became painful and heavy and Joana was a cloud about to rain. She breathed poorly as if there was no place for the air inside her. She paced back and forth, perplexed by the change. How?—she wondered and felt she was being naïve, were there two sides to it? Suffering for the same reason that had made her terribly happy?

She carried her sick body with her, an inconvenient casualty, during the day. Her lightness had been replaced with misery and weariness. Satiated—an animal that had quenched its thirst by inundating its body with water. But anxious and unhappy as if in spite of everything there was still land yet to be watered, arid and thirsty. She suffered above all from lack of understanding, alone, dumfounded. Until leaning her forehead against the windowpane (street quiet, night falling, the world out there), she realized her face was wet. She cried freely, as if it was the solution. Her tears ran thick, without her contracting a single face muscle. She cried more than she could count. Afterwards she felt as if she had returned to her true proportions, tiny, wilted, humble. Serenely empty. She was ready.

She went to him then. And the new glory and new suffering were more intense and of a more unbearable quality.

She got married.

Love came to confirm all of the old things whose existence she only knew of without ever having accepted or felt them. The world spun under her feet, there were two sexes among humans, a line connected hunger to satisfaction, animal love, rainwater headed for the sea, children were growing beings, in

the earth the sprout would become a plant. She could not longer deny … what? she wondered in suspense. The luminous
centre of things, the confirmation underpinning everything, the
harmony that existed beneath the things she didn't understand.

She rose to a new morning, sweetly alive. And her happiness was pure like the sun's reflection in the water. Each event
vibrated in her body like little crystal needles shattering. After
the short, profound moments she lived serenely for a long time,
understanding, receiving, resigning herself to everything. It felt
like she was part of the true world and had strangely distanced
herself from mankind. Although in this period she managed to
offer people her hand with a fraternity whose live source they
felt. They told her about their own woes and she, although she
didn't hear, didn't think, didn't speak, had a good gaze—shining and mysterious like that of a pregnant woman.

What was going on then? Miraculously alive, free of all
memories. The whole past had fogged over. And the present
was also mists, the sweet, cool mists that separated her from
solid reality, preventing her from touching it. If she prayed,
if she thought it would be to give thanks for having a body
made for love. The only truth became the tenderness she had
sunk into. Her face was light and imprecise, floating among the
other opaque, confident faces, as if it still couldn't find support
in any expression. All of her body and soul lost their limits,
mixed together, merged into a single chaos, soft and amorphous, slow and with vague movements like matter that was
simply alive. It was the perfect renewal, creation.

And her connection with the earth was so deep and her
certainty so firm— of what? of what?—that now she could lie
without giving herself away. All this made her think at times:

"Goodness me, what if I'm making more of this than love?"

Little by little she got used to her new state, grew accustomed to breathing, to living. Little by little she aged on the inside, opened her eyes and was a statue again, no longer pliable, but defined. Far off restlessness was being reborn. At night, between the sheets, a movement or an unexpected thought would awaken her to herself. Slightly surprised she'd dilate her eyes, perceive her body immersed in comfortable happiness. She wasn't suffering, but where was she?

"Joana … Joana …" she called herself softly. And her body barely answered slowly, quietly: "Joana."

The days sped past and she yearned to find herself more. She now called herself strongly and breathing wasn't enough for her. Happiness was erasing her, erasing her … She already wanted to feel herself again, even if it was with pain. But she sunk down further and further. Tomorrow, she put it off, tomorrow I'm going to see myself. The new day however flitted over her surface, as light as a summer afternoon, barely ruffling her nerves.

The only thing she hadn't got used to was sleeping. Sleeping was an adventure every night, falling from the easy clarity in which she lived into the same mystery, dark and cool, crossing darkness. Dying and being reborn.

I'll never have guidelines then, she thought some months after marrying. I slide from one truth to the next, always forgetting the first, always dissatisfied. Her life was made up of complete little lives, of whole, closed circles, which isolated themselves from one another. Except that at the end of each, instead of dying and beginning life on another plane, inorganic or lower organic, Joana started over on the same human plane. Just different fundamental notes. Or just different supplementary ones, and the basic ones forever the same?

It was always useless to have been happy or unhappy. And

even to have loved. No happiness or unhappiness had been so strong that it had transformed the elements of her matter, giving her a single path, as the truth path must be. I carry on always inaugurating myself, opening and closing circles of life, tossing them aside, withered, full of past. Why so independent, why don't they merge into just one block, providing me with ballast? Fact was they were too whole. Moments so intense, red, condensed in themselves that they didn't need past or future in order to exist. They brought a knowledge that didn't serve as experience—a direct knowledge, more like sensation than perception. The truth then discovered was so much the truth that it couldn't subsist except in its recipient, in the actual fact that had provoked it. So true, so fatal, that it only revolves around its matrix. Once the moment of life is over, the corresponding truth is also drained. I cannot mold it, make it inspire other instants the same as it. Nothing therefore binds me.

Yet the justification of her short glory had no other value perhaps than to give her a certain pleasure in reasoning, such as: if a rock falls, the rock exists, the rock fell from a place, the rock … She was wrong so often.

PART TWO

The Marriage

JOANA SUDDENLY REMEMBERED, WITH NO PRIOR warning, herself standing at the top of the stairs. She didn't know if she'd ever been at the top of a staircase, looking down, at lots of busy people, dressed in satin, with large fans. It was really most unlikely that she'd ever experienced it. The fans, for example, had no consistency in her memory. If she tried to think about them she didn't actually see fans, but bright smears swimming from side to side amidst words in French, whispered carefully by puckered lips, forward like a kiss sent from afar. The fan began as a fan and ended with the words in French. Absurd. It was therefore a lie.

But in spite of everything the impression kept wanting to move on, as if the main thing lay beyond the staircase and the fans. She stopped the movements for an instant and only her eyes beat quickly, searching for the feeling. Ah, yes. She walked down the marble staircase, feeling in the soles of her feet the cold fear of slipping, in her hands a hot sweat, at her waist a ribbon tightening, pulling her upwards like a light crane. Then the smell of new fabrics, a man's shiny, curious gaze piercing her and leaving her, as if it had pressed a button in the dark, her body illuminated. She was traversed by long whole muscles. Thoughts ran down these polished ropes until they quivered there, in her ankles, where the flesh was as soft as a chicken's.

She'd stop on the bottom step, wide and without danger, lightly resting the palm of her hand on the cold, smooth handrail. And without knowing why she'd feel a sudden happiness, almost painful, a languor in her heart, as if it were made of dough and someone had sunk their fingers into it, kneading it softly. Why? She fragilely lifted her hand, in a gesture of refusal. She didn't want to know. But now the question had already occurred to her and as an absurd answer came the gleaming handrail skillfully tossed from up high like a varnished streamer on a carnival day. Except that it wasn't carnival, because there was silence in the ballroom, everything could be seen through it. The moist reflections of the lamps on the mirrors, the ladies' brooches and men's belt buckles communicating at intervals with the chandelier, through slender rays of light.

More and more she understood the setting. Between the men and women there were no hard spaces, everything merged together sluggishly. From some invisible heater rose a moist, exciting vapor. Again her heart hurt slightly and she smiled, her nose wrinkled, her breathing weak.

There was a small pause for rest. She slowly started regaining reality, in spite of her effort to the contrary, her body insensitive again, opaque and strong like something that had been alive for a long time. She made out the bedroom, the curtains waving ironically, the obstinately unmoving, useless bed. Restlessly she tried to transfer herself to the top of the staircase, to walk down it again. She saw herself walking, but her legs no longer felt shaky, or her hands sweaty. Then she saw that she had emptied the memory.

She waited there, by the bookshelf, where she had gone to fetch … what? She knitted her brow without much interest. What? She tried to be amused by the feeling that in the center of her forehead there was now a hole in the place from which the idea of what she had gone to fetch had been taken.

She leaned toward the door and asked out loud, eyes closed: "What was it you wanted, Otávio?"

"The one on Civil Law," he said, and before turning his attention back to his notebook he shot her a quick look of surprise.

She took him the book, absent, her movements unhurried. He waited for it with his hand out, without lifting his head. She held back an instant with the book facing him, a short distance from him. But Otávio didn't notice her pause and with a small shoulder movement she placed it between his fingers.

She sat on a nearby chair, without making herself comfortable, as if she'd be leaving in an instant. Little by little, since nothing happened, she leaned back into the armchair and let herself go, eyes empty, without thinking.

Otávio was still in Civil Law, taking his time over one line or another and then biting his fingernail impatiently and quickly flicking back several pages at once. Until he'd stop again, distracted, tongue running over the edges of his teeth, one hand tenderly tugging on his eyebrow hairs. Some word immobilized him, hand in the air, mouth open like a dead fish. Suddenly he shoved the book away. With shiny, greedy eyes, he quickly scribbled in his notebook, stopping a moment to breathe noisily and, in a gesture that startled her, to rap on his teeth with his knuckles.

What an animal, she thought. He stopped what he was writing and looked at her in fright, as if she'd thrown something. She continued staring at him weakly and Otávio fidgeted in his chair, thinking only that he was not alone. He smiled, shy and peeved, reached his hand over the table to her. She leaned forward and offered him in turn her fingertips. Otávio gave them a quick squeeze, smiling, and then, before she'd even had time to pull her arm back, furiously returned to his notebook, his face almost sinking into it, hand working.

He was the one who was feeling now, thought Joana. And, suddenly, perhaps out of envy, without a single thought, she hated him with such brute force that her hands clamped over the arms of the chair and her teeth clenched together. She palpitated for a few instants, reanimated. Fearing her husband would sense her sharp gaze, she was forced to disguise it and thus diminish the intensity of her feeling.

It was his fault, she thought coldly, anticipating a new wave of anger. It was his fault, it was his fault. His presence, and more than his presence: knowing that he existed, took away her freedom. Only rarely now, in a quick escape, was she able to feel. That was it: it was his fault. How hadn't she discovered it earlier? she wondered victoriously. He stole everything from her, everything. And since the phrase was still weak, she thought intensely, her eyes closed, everything! She felt better, she thought with more clarity.

Before him she always had her hands out and how much oh how much did she receive by surprise! By violent surprise, like a ray, of sweet surprise, like a rain of little lights ... Now all of her time had been forfeited to him and she felt that the minutes that were hers had been ceded, split into tiny ice cubes that she had to swallow quickly, before they melted. And flogging herself to go at a gallop: look, because this time is freedom! look, think quickly, look, find yourself quickly, look ... it's over! Now—only later, the tray of ice cubes again and there you are staring at it in fascination, watching the droplets of water already trickling.

Then he'd come. And she'd finally rest, with a sigh, heavily.—But she didn't want to rest!—Her blood ran through her more slowly, its pace domesticated, like a beast that had trained its steps to fit in its cage.

She remembered when she'd gone to fetch—what was it? ah, Civil Law— on the bookshelf at the top of the staircase, such an unprompted memory, so free, imagined even … How new she was then. Clear water running inside and out. She missed the feeling, needed to feel again. She glanced anxiously from one side to the other, looking for something. But everything there was as it had been for a long time. Old. I'm going to leave him, was her first thought, unprecedented. She opened her eyes, keeping tabs on herself. She knew this thought could have consequences. At least in the past, when her resolutions didn't require big facts, just a small idea, an insignificant vision, in order to be born. I'm going to leave him, she repeated and this time the thought gave off tiny filaments binding it to her. From here on in it was inside her and the filaments would grow thicker and thicker until they formed roots.

How many more times would she propose it to herself, before she actually left him? She grew tired in advance of the small struggles she was yet to have, rebelling and then giving in, until the end. She had a quick, impatient internal movement that was only reflected in an imperceptible lifting of her hand. Otávio glanced at her for a second and continued writing like a sleepwalker. How sensitive he was, she thought in an interval. She kept going: why put it off? Yes, why put it off? she asked herself. And her question was solid, demanding a serious answer. She straightened up in her chair, adopted a ceremonious position, as if to hear what she had to say.

Then Otávio sighed loudly, noisily snapped the book and notebook shut, flung them away, exaggeratedly, his long legs stretched out far from the chair. She looked at him in surprise, offended. So ... she began with irony. But she didn't know how to go on and waited, staring at him.

He said, with a comical air of severity:

"Very well. Now would her lady be so kind as to come over here and lean her head against this valiant chest, because I need it."

She laughed, just to satisfy him. But in the middle of the laugh she'd already found it a bit funny. She remained seated, trying to go on: So, he ... and she made an expression of distain and victory with her lips, as if receiving the proof she had expected. So, he ... Was that it? She hoped Otávio would note her stance, divine her resolution not to budge from the chair. He, however, as always, divined nothing and precisely at the moments in which he should have looked, was distracted by something. Now, right now, he'd remembered to straighten up the book and notebook he'd tossed across the table. He didn't even look at Joana, was he certain she'd come? She laughed an evil laugh, thinking how mistaken he was and how many thoughts she'd had without his even imagining it. Yes, why put it off?

He looked up, a little surprised at how long she was taking. And since she was still in her chair, they sat there staring at one another from afar. He was intrigued.

"So?" he said half-heartedly. "My valiant ..."

Joana interrupted him with a gesture, because she couldn't stand the pity that had suddenly invaded her and the impression of how ridiculous the phrase was, when she herself was so lucid and determined to speak. He was unfazed by her movement and she had to carefully swallow her saliva in order to push down into herself the stupid desire to cry that was starting to be born mushy in her chest.

Now her pity encompassed her too and she saw the two of them together, pitiful and childish. They were both going to die, the same man who had rapped on his teeth with his knuckles, in such an alive movement. She herself, with the top of the stairs and all of her capacity to want to feel. The main things assaulted her at any old time, in the in-between moments too, filling them with meanings. How many times had she tipped the waiter more than necessary just because she'd remembered that he was going to die and didn't know it.

She looked at him mysteriously, serious and tender. And now she tried to be moved thinking about the two future dead people.

She leaned her head against his chest and there a heart was beating. She thought: but even so, in spite of death, I'm going to leave him one day. She was all too familiar with the thought that might come to her, strengthening her, if she was moved before leaving him: "I took everything I could have. I don't hate him, I don't look down on him. Why go to him, even if you love him? I don't like myself that much that I like the things I like. I love what I want more than myself." Oh, she knew just as well that the truth might lie in the opposite of what she'd thought. She relaxed her head, pressed her forehead into Otávio's white shirt. Slowly, very subtly, the idea of death disappeared and she no longer found anything to laugh at. Her heart was softly molded. With her ear she knew that Otávio, oblivious to everything, carried on in his regular beats, on his fatal path. The sea.

"Put it off, just put it off," thought Joana before she stopped thinking. Because the last ice cubes had melted and now she was sadly a happy woman.

Refuge in the Teacher

JOANA REMEMBERED WELL: DAYS BEFORE HER WEDding she had gone to see her teacher.

She had suddenly needed to see him, to feel him firm and cold before leaving. Because she somehow felt like she was betraying all of her past life by marrying. She wanted to see the teacher again, feel his support. And when the idea to visit him had come to her, she felt relieved.

He would surely give her the right word. What word? Nothing, she answered herself mysteriously, wanting in a sudden yearning for faith and good hope to preserve herself in order to hear him completely new, without the slightest idea of what she'd get. It had already happened to her once: when she was preparing to go to the circus for the first time, as a girl. She had her best moments getting ready for it. And when she drew near the wide field where the tent gleamed white, round and immense like one of those domes that hide the best dish on the table until a certain moment, when she drew near holding the maid's hand, she felt the fear and the anxiety and the tremulous joy in her heart and wanted to turn back, run away.

When the maid said: your father sent money for popcorn, Joana looked at things perplexed, under the afternoon full of sun, as if they were crazy.

She knew that the teacher had taken ill, that his wife had left him. But although he had aged, she found him fatter, a sparkle in his eye. She had also feared at first that their last scene in common, when she had fled to her puberty in fright, might make the visit difficult, put them ill at ease, in that same strange, deceptive room where the dust had now won out over the shine.

The teacher received her with a serene, absent-minded air. The dark circles under his eyes made him look like an old photograph. He asked Joana questions and no sooner had she begun to answer than he'd stop listening, as if finally relieved of the obligation. He interrupted himself several times, his attention trained on the clock and the little table where his medicine was. She glanced around and the half darkness was moist and panting. The teacher was like a large neutered cat reigning over a cellar.

"Now you can open the windows," he said. "You know, a little darkness and then lots of air; the whole body benefits, receives life. It's like a neglected child. When they receive everything, they suddenly react, blossom again, more than the others, sometimes."

Joana flung open the windows and doors and the cold air entered in a triumphant gust. A little sunlight was coming through the door behind him. The teacher loosened the collar of his pajamas, exposed himself to the wind.

"That's it," he declared.

Looking at him Joana realized he was just a fat old man in the sun, his thinning hair unable to resist the breeze, his large body draped over the chair. And the smile, my God, a smile.

When the clock struck three, he suddenly stirred, stopped mid-sentence and, with measured gestures, his face avid and grave, counted twenty drops from a vial into a glass of water. He raised it to eye-level, observing it, lips pressed closed, entirely absorbed. He drank the dark liquid without fear, then stared at the glass with a bitter face and a half-smile that she was unable to explain. He placed it on the table, clapped his hands to call the servant, a thin, absent-minded kid. He waited in silence for him to return, his gaze alert as if trying to hear from afar. Only when he had received the washed glass back, examined it closely and turned it upside down on a saucer, did he give a light sigh:

"Anyway, what were we talking about?"

She continued not paying attention to her own words, observing him. No feature of the man's face gave away his wife's leaving him. Fugitively she saw in her mind's eye that almost always silent figure, with her impassive, sovereign face, whom she had feared and hated. And, in spite of the repulsion that the wife still inspired in her, recollecting, Joana realized with surprise that not only then, but perhaps always, she had felt united with her, as if they both had something secret and evil in common.

Nothing in his appearance betrayed his wife's departure. In fact it was as if he had at long last acquired a tranquility in his demeanor and gaze, a state of repose that Joana had never noticed in him before. She scrutinized him almost distraught like the waters swollen by the rain whose depth was now impossible to gauge. She had come to hear him, to feel his lucidity as a stationary point!

"A strong man's torture is greater than a sick man's," she said, trying to get him to speak.

He barely looked up. Her phrase hung in the air, foolish and timid. I shall proceed, it is precisely my nature to never feel ridiculous, I take my chances always, I walk onto all stages. Otávio, on the contrary, with such a fragile esthetic that all it takes is a sharper laugh to break it and make him miserable. He would hear me now restlessly or else smiling. Was Otávio already thinking inside her? Had she already become the kind of woman who listens to and waits for her man? She was giving something up … She wanted to save herself, to hear the teacher, to shake him. So didn't the old man in front of her remember everything he'd told her? 'To sin against yourself …'

"The sick imagine the world and the able-bodied own it," Joana went on. "The sick don't think they can just because they are infirm and the strong feel their strength is useless."

Yes, yes, he nodded, shy. She realized that her discomfort was only that of one who doesn't want to be interrupted. She continued until the end however, her dead voice repeating the thought from so long ago.

"That is why the poetry of the poets who have suffered is sweet, tender. And that of the others, of those who have never been deprived, is blazing, suffering and rebellious."

"Yes," he said adjusting the loose collar of his pajamas.

Humiliated and perplexed she saw his dark, wrinkled neck. Yes, he said from time to time without his attention, seeking support, ever straying from the clock. How to tell him she was going to get married?

At four o'clock the ritual was repeated. This time the kid dodged a kick, because he almost dropped the medicine vial. With his frustrated attempt, the teacher's slipper flew off and his foot with curling yellow nails appeared naked. The boy picked up the slipper and tossed it to Joana, laughing, afraid to get any closer. After the glass had been stowed away, she ventured her first words about his illness, slowly, ashamed, because they had never before entered the intimacy of their personal experiences, they had always understood one another outside of themselves.

She didn't need to push any further ... He began to steer the subject, caressing it slowly, explaining it to her in detail unhurriedly and with pleasure. He was somewhat obliging and mysterious at first, not believing it possible that she would enter his world. But after a few moments, forgetting her presence, gently enthused, he was already speaking openly.

"The doctor said I'm still not better. But I'm going to get well, I know more than all the doctors," he added. "After all if I'm the sick man ..."

She finally realized, astonished, that he was happy ...

It was nearly five o'clock. She sensed that he was eager for her to leave. But she wasn't going to leave him like that, and again tried to push herself. She looked him straight in the eye, cruelly. He met her gaze with indifferent, lukewarm eyes at first and immediately afterwards balked in anger, irritated.

The Little Family

BEFORE HE STARTED WRITING, OTÁVIO WOULD METIC-
ulously order his papers on the table, straighten his clothes on
himself. He liked small gestures and old habits, like worn garments, where he moved about seriously and safely. Ever since
his student days he had prepared to work in this manner. After
installing himself at the table, he would tidy it and, his awareness reawakened by the notion of the things around him (I
shan't lose myself in big ideas, I am a thing too), he'd allow his
pen to run a little freely in order to rid himself of a persistent
image or idea that may have decided to dog him and stanch
his main stream of thought.

For this reason working in front of other people was torture. He feared he'd be ridiculed for his little rituals and yet he
couldn't do without them, they provided as much support as
a superstition. Just as in order to live he surrounded himself
with permissions and taboos, formulas and concessions. Everything became easier, as he'd been taught. What fascinated
and terrified him about Joana was precisely the freedom in
which she lived, suddenly loving certain things or blind to

others, without using them at all. But Otávio found himself obligated to in the face of what existed. It was just as Joana had said, he needed to be owned by someone … "You handle money with such intimacy …" Joana had once joked as he was paying the bill at a restaurant and had caught him so distracted that she had startled him and, in front of the waiter, no doubt ironic, the bills and coins had slipped from his hands and scattered at his feet. Although there was no ironic comment following it—well, truth be told, Joana doesn't laugh—he'd still had an argument ready ever since: but what else should one do with money but save it in order to spend it? He felt irritated, ashamed. He felt that the argument didn't respond to Joana.

The truth is that if he didn't have money, if he didn't own the "conventionals," if he didn't love order, if the Law Magazine didn't exist, the vague plan for the book on civil law, if Lídia weren't separate to Joana, if Joana wasn't a woman and he a man, if … oh, God, if everything … what would he do? No, not "what would he do," but whom would he address, how would he move? It was impossible to slip between the blocks, without seeing them, without needing them …

Contravening his work rule (a concession), he took up pencil and paper before he was entirely prepared. But he forgave himself, he didn't want to let the observation slip, it might come in handy one day: "A certain degree of blindness is necessary in order to see certain things. This is perhaps the mark of an artist. Any man might know more than him and safely reason, according to the truth. But those things in particular cannot be seen with the light on. In the darkness they become phosphorescent." —He thought a little. Then, although his concession had already gone on too long, he scribbled: "It is not the degree that separates intelligence from genius, but the quality. Genius isn't so much a question of intellectual power, but of the form in which this power presents itself. As such one can easily be more intelligent than a genius. But the genius is him. This 'the genius is him' is childish. See whether Spinoza's discovery applies." — Was it his? Every idea that occurred to him, because he became familiar with it in seconds, came with the fear of having stolen it.

Well, now order. Pencil down, he told himself, free yourself of obsessions. One, two, three! I dearly lament suffering as I do amidst the bamboo in the northwest of this city, he began. I do what I want, he went on, and no one is making me write the Divine Comedy. There is nothing else to be but what you are, the rest is useless embroidery and as uncomfortable as the one, in relief, with angels and flowers, that cousin Isabel used to decorate my pillows. When I was lost in thought and she'd come along like a stupid purple cloud, what was I thinking, tell me what, tell me what, what, four more times what, what, what, what. Like that, like that, don't avoid it: "what? you're still alive? you haven't died yet?" Yes, yes, that was it, don't avoid myself, don't avoid my handwriting, how light and horrible it is, a spider's web, don't avoid my flaws, my flaws, I love you, my qualities are so small, the same as those of other men, my flaws, my negative side is beautiful and concave like an abyss. What I am not would leave an enormous hole in the earth. I don't nourish my errors, while Joana doesn't err, there's the difference. Hey, hey, say something, young man. Women look at me, women, women, my mouth, I let my moustache grow again, they swoon with happiness and great love, full of plums and raisins. I buy them all without money, money I save, if one of them slips on a peel out in the street, there's naught to do but feel ashamed. Nothing lost, nothing created. The man who felt this, that is, who didn't just understand, but adored it, would be as happy as he who really believes in God. In the beginning it hurts a little, but then you get used to it. He who is writing this page was born one day. Now it is exactly a little past seven in the morning. There are mists outside, beyond the window, the Open Window, the great symbol. Joana would say: I feel so inside the world that it feels like I'm not thinking, but using a new means of breathing. Farewell. This is the world, I am me, it is raining in the world, it's a lie, I'm an intellectual worker, Joana is asleep in the bedroom, somebody must be waking up now, Joana would say: someone else dying, someone else listening to music, someone walked into a bathroom, that's the world. I'm going to touch everyone, invite them to be moved by me. I live with a naked, cold woman, don't avoid it, don't avoid it, who looks me right in the eye, don't avoid it, who watches me, it's a lie, it's a lie, but it's true. Now she is lying down sleeping, she has been defeated by sleep, defeated, defeated. She's a slight bird in a white nightdress. I'm going to move everyone, I don't nourish my errors, but may they all nourish me.

He straightened his torso, smoothed his hair, grew serious. Now he was going to work. As if everyone was watching and nodding approvingly, closing their eyes in their assent: yes, that's right, very good. Someone real was bothering him and on his own he became unstuck, nervous. For "everyone" was watching him. He coughed slightly. He carefully pushed away the inkwell. He began. "The modern tragedy is man's vain attempt to adapt to the state of things that he has created."

He distanced himself a little, looked at his notebook, straightened his pajamas. "Man is so deeply based in the imagination—Joana again—that the entire world he has built finds its justification in the beauty of creation and not in its usefulness, not in being the result of a plan with ends adequate to its needs. This is why we see a multiplication of remedies designed to unite man with existing ideas and institutions — education, for example, so difficult — and we see him remain always on the outside of the world he has built. Man raises houses to look at rather than to live in. Because everything follows the path of inspiration. Determinism isn't a determinism of ends, but a narrow determinism of causes. Playing, inventing, following the ant to the anthill, mixing water with lime to see the result, this is what you do when you are little and when you are big. It is a mistake to think we have arrived at a high degree of pragmatism and materialism. In fact pragmatism — a plan aimed at a real given end — would be comprehension, stability, happiness, the biggest victory of adaptation that man could achieve. However doing things "so that" strikes me, faced with reality, as a degree of perfection impossible to expect of man. His entire body of work begins "because." Curiosity, fancy, imagination — these are what have shaped the modern world. Following inspiration, he mixed ingredients, created combinations. His tragedy: to have to nourish himself with them. He trusted that he could imagine in one life and exist in another, separate one. This other one really does go on, but its purification over the imagined works slowly and a lone man doesn't find foolish thinking on one side and the peace of the true life on the other. One cannot think with impunity." Joana thought without fear and without punishment. Would she end up mad or what? He had no idea. Perhaps only suffering.

He stopped, reread it. To not leave this world, he thought with a certain ardor. To not have to face the rest. To just think, to just think and write it down. Would that he be asked to write articles about Spinoza, but that he wasn't obliged to practice law, to look at and deal with those affrontingly human people, parading, exposing their lives shamelessly.

He reread his notes on his previous reading.—The pure scientist stops believing in what he likes, but cannot stop himself from liking what he believes. The need to like: the mark of man.—Don't forget: "the intellectual love of God" is the true knowledge and precludes any mysticism or adoration.—Many answers are to be found in Spinoza's statements. For example in the idea that there cannot be thought without extension (a mode of God) and vice-versa, isn't the mortality of the soul affirmed? Of course: mortality as a distinct, reasoning soul, the clear impossibility of the pure form of St. Thomas' angels. Mortality as regards the human. Immortality through transformation in nature.—Within the world there is no place for other creations. There is just an opportunity for reintegration and continuity. Everything that could exist already exists. Nothing else can be created but revealed.—If, the more evolved the man, the more he tries to summarize, evaluate and establish principles and laws for his life, how could God— in any sense, even the conscious God of the religions—not have absolute laws as a result of his own perfection? A God endowed with free will is lesser than a God of one law. The same way a concept is so much truer the more it is one only and doesn't need to transform with each particular instance. God's perfection is proven more by the impossibility of miracles than by their possibility. To work miracles, for a humanized God of the religions, is to be unfair —thousands of people need miracles equally and at the same time—or to recognize an error, correcting it—which, more than kindness or "proof of character," means an error was made.—Neither understanding or volition are part of God's nature, says Spinoza. This makes me happier and freer. Because the idea of the existence of a conscious God is horribly dissatisfying.

At the top of the study he'd put Spinoza translated *in litteris*: "Bodies are distinguished from one another in respect of motion and rest, quickness and slowness, and not by reason of their substance." He had shown the sentence to Joana. What for? He shrugged, without seeking any further explanation. She had been curious, had wanted to read the book.

Otávio reached out his hand and picked it up. A page from a notebook was tucked between its pages. He looked at it and discovered Joana's uncertain handwriting. He leaned over it avidly. "The beauty of the words: God's abstract nature. It is like listening to Bach." Why did he wish she hadn't written that? Joana always caught him off guard. He felt ashamed as if she were clearly lying and he was obliged to trick her, telling her that he believed her ...

Reading what she had written was like being in front of Joana. He conjured her up and, avoiding her eyes, saw her in her moments of distraction, her face white, vague and light. And suddenly great melancholy descended over him. What exactly am I doing? he wondered and didn't even know why he had attacked himself so suddenly. No, don't write today. And because this was a concession, an order not to be questioned—he scrutinized himself: if he sincerely wanted to could he work? and the answer was resolute: no—and since the decision was more powerful than him, he felt almost happy. Today someone was giving him time off. Not God. Not God, but someone. Very strong.

He'd get up, straighten his papers, put the book away, put on some warm clothes, go see Lídia. The comfort of Order. How would he be received by Lídia? Before the open window, watching children walk to school, he saw himself grab her shoulders, in a sudden rage, perhaps a little contrived, confronted with that same question: what exactly am I doing?

"Aren't you afraid?" he'd shouted at her.

Lídia had remained the same.

"Aren't you afraid of your future, of our future, of me? Don't you know that … that … being merely my lover … your only place is by my side?"

She had shaken her head surprised, tearful:

"But no …"

He had shaken her, vaguely ashamed to show so much force, when in Joana's company, for example, he kept quiet.

"Aren't you afraid I'll leave you? Don't you know that if I leave you, you'll be a woman without a husband, without anything … A sorry wretch … who's fiancée left her one day and who became this fiancée's lover while he married another woman …"

"I don't want you to leave me …"

"Ah …"

" …but I'm not afraid …"

He had looked at her in surprise. She was losing weight, he noticed. But she still looked healthy. In spite of everything more nervous, quick to tears, to be moved. Suddenly he started to laugh.

"I don't know what you are made of, I swear."

Lídia had laughed too, pleased that it was all over. He had been intimidated by her radiant look, pulled her to him so he wouldn't see her eyes. And they stood there a moment in an embrace, full of different desires.

And now? Lídia would receive him as always. He wrote a note to Joana, telling her he wouldn't be home for lunch. Poor

Joana ..., he could say if he wanted to. She'd never know. So upstanding in her oblivious loftiness ... But he would fiercely spare her, he laughed, his heart beating. Anyhow, tomorrow he'd write something definitive about the article.

He looked himself in the mirror before leaving, with squinting eyes he observed his well-formed face, straight nose, round, fleshy lips. But at the end of the day I am guilty of nothing, he said. Not even of having been born. And suddenly he didn't understand how he'd been able to believe in responsibility, to feel that constant weight, all the time. He was free ... How simple everything became sometimes ...

He went out, took his time choosing a bag of bonbons. He ended up buying a fairly large bag of apricot ones. When he turned the corner, he'd suck on his first bonbon, hands in pockets. His eyes filled with tenderness thinking about it. Why not? he asked himself suddenly irritated. Who said great men don't eat bonbons? Except that in biographies no one remembers to mention it. What if Joana knew about this thought of his? No, actually she had never shown sarcasm at ... He had a moment of anger, quickened his step.

Before he turned the corner, he took the bag of bonbons and dumped them in the gutter. Distressed, he watched as they mixed into the mud, rolled into a dark hollow crisscrossed with spider webs.

He continued on his way more slowly, withdrawn. It was a little cold out. Now someone must be satisfied, he thought remotely. Like a punishment, a confession.

"Even great men are only truly recognized and paid homage after they are dead. Why? Because those who praise need to feel in some way superior to the person receiving the praise, they need to grant it. After ... an evident superiority is born ...

those who praise … managed to remain … there's even a certain condescension … left … pity," Otávio was saying.

Lídia was observing him in one of his ugly moments. Thin lips, wrinkled forehead, dumb stare—Otávio was thinking. And she loved him in this instant. His ugliness didn't excite her, didn't inspire pity. She simply became even more attached to him and with greater happiness. Happiness to accept entirely, to feel that she was uniting what was true and primitive in herself with someone, regardless of any received ideas about beauty. She remembered her former classmates—those eternally quick-witted girls, who knew everything, having connections with cinemas, books, dating, clothes, those young ladies she had never really been able to get close to, quiet as she was, without actually having something to say. She remembered them and knew that they would have found Otávio ugly at that moment. Because she accepted him so much that she would desire him worse to prove her love without a fight even more.

She looked at him without paying attention to his words. It was sweet and good to know that between the two of them there were secrets weaving a fine, light life over the other life, the real one. No one would ever guess that Otávio had kissed her on the eyelids once, that he had felt her eyelashes on his lips and that it had made him smile. And miraculously she had understood everything without them speaking. No one would know that they had once wanted each other so much that they had remained silent, serious, unmoving. Inside each of them knowledge never scrutinized by others was piling up. He had left one day. But it didn't matter so much. She knew that between them there were "secrets," that both were irremediably accomplices. If he left, if he loved another woman, he'd leave and love another woman only to share it with her afterwards, even if he told her nothing. Lídia would take part in his life anyway. Certain things don't happen without consequence, she thought gazing at him. Flee—and you'll never be free … Once she had tripped, he had held her, straightened her hair in an absent-minded gesture. She thanked him with a little squeeze of the arm. They had looked at once another with a smile and suddenly felt blindingly happy … They had quickened their pace, open eyes dazzled.

He may not have remembered that in particular. She was the one with the memory for that kind of thing. Actually, the quality of these incidents was such, that you couldn't remember them by speaking. Or even by thinking in words. The only way was to stop for a moment and feel it again. Let him forget. In his soul, however, there would be some kind of mark, light, pink, keeping note of the feeling of that afternoon. As for her—each day that arrived brought her in its waters more memories with which to nourish herself. And little by little a certainty of happiness, of goal achieved, slowly rose up through her body, leaving her satisfied, almost satiated, almost anxious. Whenever she saw Otávio again she looked at him now without any great emotion, thinking him inferior to what he had given her. She wanted to tell him about her happiness. But she was vaguely afraid of hurting him, as if she were telling him she had cheated on him with another man. Or as if she wanted to flaunt her happiness (to he who divided himself between two houses and two women), to show that it was superior to his.

Yes, she thought distantly, staring at him—there are indestructible things that accompany the body to death as if they had been born with it. And one of them is what is created between a man and a woman who have experienced certain moments together.

And when her child was born—she caressed her belly which was already beginning to bulge—the three of them would be a little family. She thought in words: a little family. That was what she wanted. Like a good ending to her whole story. She and Otávio had been brought up together, by their cousin in common. She had lived close to Otávio. No one had passed through her life but him. In him she had discovered the man, before she knew about men and women. Without reasoning, confusedly, Otávio was the whole species to her. She lived him so fully that she had never felt others except as closed, strange, superficial worlds. Always, in all of her phases, near him. Even in that period in which she'd become crafty, hiding everything she could, even what she didn't need to hide. Even in the next one, in which people looked at her in the street, her classmates accepted her admiring her beautiful, thick hair. Otávio following her with his eyes … that certainty, never again erased, that she was someone … That was when she understood that she wasn't poor, that she had something to give Otávio, that there was a way to dedicate her life to him, everything she had been … She had waited for him. When she had attained him, Joana had come along and he had fled. She kept waiting. He returned. A child would be born. Yes, but before it was born she would demand her rights. She felt that the phrase "demand her rights" had lain inside her forever, waiting. Waiting for her to have the strength. She wished the child would sprout between its parents. And at the bottom of it all, she wanted "the little family" for herself.

She smiled slightly, listening to Otávio descant about something or other of which she couldn't make head or tail. Ever since the fetus had begun to form inside her, she had lost certain tics, gained others, and dared advance in certain thoughts.

She felt as if she had lived a lie until then. Her movements were freer from her body, as if now there was more space in the world for her being. She would take care of the child and Otávio, yes she would … She settled back better in the arm-chair, her embroidery slid onto the rug. She half-closed her eyes and her belly grew like that, bountiful, shiny. She suc-cumbed to well-being, a certain laziness that came over her frequently now. She hadn't had the slightest morning sickness, not even at the beginning. And she knew that the birth would be simple, simple like everything. She placed her hand on her flanks that were still not deformed. She somehow looked down on other women considerably.

Otávio caught the expression, surprised. An absent-minded cruelty … He studied her, unable to decipher it, understand-ing only that he was excluded from that half smile. Because it was a smile, a horrible smile, gloating, even though her face remained serious, her eyes open, looking straight ahead. Fear struck him, he almost shouted:

"You weren't even listening!"

Lídia sat forward in the chair with a start, once again his, once again devoted:

"I …"

"You didn't even understand me at least," he repeated star-ing at her, his breathing oppressed. Was the scene from the last time going to repeat itself? No, there was a child in her. Why am I going to have a child? Why me? Precisely me? It's strange … In an instant he'd ask himself: what exactly am I doing? No, no …

"But I do more than understand you," she said quickly, "I love you …"

He sighed imperceptibly, still a little rattled by her escape.

Truth was, she didn't fully come back anymore, as she had before the pregnancy. And he had given her the kingdom himself, the fool ... Yes, but when she was free of the child, when she was free of the child ... A few minutes later, calm again, Otávio allowed himself to be invaded by the abandon and lassitude that sustained his relations with Lídia so well.

The Encounter With Otávio

THE DENSE, DARK NIGHT WAS CUT DOWN THE MIDDLE, split into two black blocks of sleep. Where was she? Between the two pieces, looking at them (the one she had already slept and the one she had yet to sleep), isolated in the timeless and the spaceless, in an empty gap. This stretch would be subtracted from her years of life.

The ceiling and walls joined without corners, silent, arms folded, and she was inside a cocoon. Joana observed it without thoughts, without emotion, a thing looking at another thing. Slowly, from a leg movement, wakefulness was distantly born mixed with a taste of sleep in her mouth, then spread throughout her body. The moonlight paled the room, the bed. A moment, another moment, another moment, another moment. Suddenly, like a little ray, something lit up inside her, without moving a single face muscle she said quickly: look to your side. She kept staring at the ceiling, apparently not at all interested, but her heart beating scared. Look to your side. She figured she'd end up looking, knowing vaguely what was next to her, but she acted as if she didn't intend to, as if she was unaware of the rest of the bed. Look to your side. Then defeated, before a multitude of faces watching the scene over on the stage, she slowly turned her head on the pillow and took a peek. There was a man. She understood that she had expected exactly that.

His naked chest, his arms open, crucified. She settled her head back into its former position. There, I looked. But immediately afterwards she lifted up and leaning on her elbow stared at him, without curiosity perhaps, but demanding, waiting for an answer. Or did she do it because the impassive faces were expecting this gesture? There was a man. Who was he? The question was born light, already lost, carried along like a poor leaf by the dark waves. But before Joana could forget it entirely, she saw it grow in importance, present itself as new and urgent, the voice leaning over her: who was he?

She grew impatient, tired of the insistence of the crowd of faces that, instead of playing at directing, was now demanding, demanding. Who was he? A man, a male, she answered. But her man, that stranger. She looked him in the face, the tired face of a sleeping child. His lips parted. His pupils, under his thick descended eyelids, staring inwards, dead. She touched him lightly on the shoulder and before she had even received any kind of impression, drew back quickly, frightened. She stopped a little, feeling her own heart echo in her chest. She straightened her nightdress, giving herself time to back away if she still wanted to. But she continued. She placed her pale arm near the creature's naked arm and, although she already anticipated the thought that followed, she shivered touched by the violent difference in color, as firm and audacious as a scream. There were two delimited bodies on the bed. And this time she couldn't complain that she had made her way consciously to tragedy: the thought had imposed itself without her having chosen it. What if he woke up and found her leaning over him? If he opened his eyes suddenly, they would find themselves so face-to-face with hers, the two lights crossing paths with the other two lights ... She withdrew quickly, shrank back inside herself, full of fear, of her unconfessed dread of the rainless nights of old, in the darkness wide awake. How many times will I have to live through the same things in different situations? She imagined those eyes like two copper plates, shining without expression. What voice might come out of that sleeping throat? Sounds like thick arrows, burying themselves in the furniture, in the walls, in Joana herself softly. And everyone with folded arms too, gaze sweeping the space faraway. Relentlessly. A clock's chiming only ends when it ends, there is naught to be done. Either that or throw a rock at it, and after the noise of broken glass and springs, silence spilling out like blood. Why not kill the man? Nonsense, this thought was entirely forged. She looked at him. Fear that "it" all, like when a button is pressed—to touch him would be enough—would start working noisily, mechanically, filling the room with movements and sounds, living. She was afraid of her own fear, which isolated her. From afar, from atop the switched-off lamp, she saw herself, lost and tiny, covered in moons, beside the man who could come to life at any moment.

And suddenly, treacherously, she had a real fear, as alive as living things. The unknown that existed in that animal that was hers, in that man whom she had only known how to love! Fear in her body, fear in her blood! Maybe he'd strangle her, murder her ... Why not?—she thought with a start—the audacity with which her own thoughts advanced, guiding her like a moving, shaky little light through the dark. Where was it going? But why wouldn't Otávio strangle her? Weren't they alone? What if he was crazy under sleep?—She shivered. She had an involuntary movement with her legs, pulled back the sheets, ready to defend herself, to run ... Ah, if she screamed she wouldn't be afraid, her fear would run away with the scream ... Otávio responded to her movement raising in turn his eyebrows, pressing his lips closed, opening them again and remaining dead to the world! She looked at him, looked at him ... waited ...

No, he wasn't dangerous. She ran the back of her hand across her forehead.

There was still the silence, the same silence.

Maybe, who knows, she had experienced a little bit of dream mixed with reality, she thought. She tried to remember the past day. Nothing important, except Otávio's note telling her he wouldn't be home for lunch, as had been happening almost regularly, for some time. Or had her fear been more than a hallucination? The room was now distinct and cold. She rested with closed eyes. Fortunately her nights of bad dreams were rare.

How foolish she had been. She reached her hand over, tried to touch him. She left her palm lying on his chest, at first lightly, almost floating, but slowly subsiding. After gaining confidence from moment to moment, she abandoned it entirely on that broad field covered with light vegetation. Eyes open, unseeing, all of her attention focused on herself and what she was feeling.

There was a creak of furniture, shadows gripped the wardrobe more firmly.

Then an idea came to her. An idea so hot that her heart accompanied it with strong blows. Like this: she moved closer to him, carefully nestled her head against his arm, next to his chest. She lay still, waiting. Little by little she felt the stranger's heat transmitting itself to her through the back of her neck. She heard the rhythmic, faraway, serious beating of a heart. She examined herself keenly. That living being was hers. That stranger, that other world was hers. She saw him from afar, from atop the lamp, his naked body—lost and weak. Weak. How fragile and delicate were his uncovered lines, without protection. He, him, the man. From a hidden source anxiety came surging up through her body, filling all of her cells, pushing her desolate to the bottom of the bed. My God, my God. Afterwards, in painful labor, under difficult breathing, she felt the soft oil of surrender spill through her, at last, at last. He was hers.

She wanted to call to him, to ask for his support, to ask him to say pacifying words. But she didn't want to wake him. She feared he didn't know how to make her rise to a higher feeling, to the realization of that which at present was still a sweet embryo. She knew that even in this moment she was alone, that the man would wake up distant. That he could intercept with a block—an absent-minded, lukewarm word—the narrow, glowing path where she was taking her first stumbling steps. Nevertheless imagining him oblivious to what was going on inside her didn't diminish her tenderness. It increased it, made it bigger than her body and her soul as if to compensate for the man's distance.

Joana was smiling, but she couldn't stop the suffering from starting to palpitate through her body, like a bitter thirst. More than suffering, a desire for love growing and dominating her. Inside a vague, light whirlwind, like a quick spell of dizziness, an awareness of the world came to her, of her own life, of the past before her birth, of the future beyond her body. Yes, lost like a dot, a dot without dimensions, once, a thought. She had been born, she would die, the earth … The feeling was swift, deep: a blind plunge into a color—red, as serene and broad as a field. The same violent, instantaneous awareness that assailed her at times in great moments of love, like a drowning man seeing for the last time.

"My …" she began in a low voice.

But everything she could say wasn't enough. She was living, living. She watched him. How he slept, how he existed. She had never felt him so much. When she had joined him in marriage, in the early days, her enchantment had come to her from her own discovered body. The renewal had been hers, she hadn't overflowed to the man and had remained isolated. Now she suddenly understood that love could make you desire the next moment in an impulse that was life …—She felt the world palpitate softly in her chest, her body hurt as if she bore the femininity of all women in it.

She silenced again looking inside herself. She remembered: I am the light wave that has no other field but the sea, I thrash about, slide, fly, laughing, giving, sleeping, but woe is me, always in me, always in me. When was that from? Had she read it as a child? Thought it? Suddenly she remembered: she had thought it just now, perhaps before placing her own arm next to Otávio's, perhaps in that moment in which she had wanted to scream … More and more everything was past … And the past as mysterious as the future …

Yes … and she had also seen, quickly like a silent car speeding off, the man she ran into sometimes in the street … the man who stared at her in silence, thin and sharp as a knife. She had already felt him that night lightly, touching her awareness like a pinhead … like a forewarning … but in which moment?

In her dream? In her vigil? A new flux of pain and life welled up, inundated her, with the anxiety of imprisonment.

"I …" she began again to Otávio.

It was darker, all she could see of him was a shadow. He was fading more and more, slipping through her hands, dead at the bottom of sleep. And she, as solitary as the ticking of a clock in an empty house. She sat waiting on the bed, eyes enlarged, the cold of the approaching dawn passing through her fine shirt. Alone in the world, crushed by the excess of life, feeling the music vibrate too high for a body.

But liberation came and Joana shook with its impulse … Because, as mild and sweet as daybreak in a wood, inspiration was born … Then she made up what she should say. Eyes closed, surrendered, she softly spoke words born in that instant, never before heard by anyone, still tender from their creation—fragile, new shoots. They were less than words, just loose, meaningless, warm syllables that flowed and merged, were fertilized and reborn in a single being only to break apart immediately afterwards, breathing, breathing …

Her eyes grew moist with soft happiness and gratitude. She had spoken … The words coming from before language, from the source, from the source itself. She moved closer to him, giving him her soul and nevertheless feeling complete as if she had drunk down a world. She was like a woman.

The dark trees in the garden were secretly watching the silence, she just knew, she just knew … She fell asleep.

Lídia

THE NEXT MORNING WAS LIKE A FIRST DAY AGAIN,
felt Joana.

Otávio had left early and she blessed him for it as if he had
intentionally granted her time to think, to observe herself. She
didn't want to make any rushed decisions, feeling that any one
of her movements could become precious and dangerous.

They were instants, quick hours only. Because she received
Lídia's note inviting her to pay her a visit.

Reading it had made Joana smile even before it had brought
on that fast, heavy beating of her heart. And also the cold steel
blade pressing on the warm interior of her body. As if her dead
aunt had risen up and was speaking to her, Joana imagined
her shock, felt her eyes open (or was it her own eyes that she
didn't allow surprises?): "Did Otávio go back to Lídia, in spite
of Joana?" her aunt would say.

Joana slowly stroked her hair, the cold blade touching her
warm heart, smiled again, oh just to stall for time. "But yes, why
not stay with Lídia?" she answered her dead aunt. The blade
now, with this clear thought, pressed on her lungs laughing,

icy. Why refuse the things that happened? Have lots at the same time, feel in a number of ways, recognize life in a range of sources ... Who could stop someone from living amply?

Later she fell into a strange, light state of excitement. She drifted through the house aimlessly, even cried a bit, without great suffering, just for the sake of crying—she convinced herself—simply, like someone waving their hand, like someone looking. Am I suffering? she'd ask herself from time to time and again the person thinking filled all of her with surprise, curiosity and pride and there was no room left for someone to suffer. But her fine exaltation didn't allow her to stay on the same plane for very long. She quickly changed to a different tone of behavior, played a little piano, forgot Lídia's letter. When she remembered it, vaguely, a bird that comes and goes, she couldn't make up her mind, whether she should be sad or happy, calm or agitated. She kept remembering the previous night, the raised window pane shining serenely in the moonlight, Otávio's naked chest, Joana sleeping deeply, almost for the first time in her life, trusting herself to a man who was asleep beside her. In fact she hadn't distanced herself from the previous day's Joana full of tenderness. Ashamed, humbled and rejected, that Joana had wandered about until she returned and was increasingly tough, more focused and closer to herself—she thought. All the better. Except that the cold steel was always renewed, never warmed. More than anything, at the bottom of any thought hovered another, perplexed, almost enchanted, like the day her father died: things happened without her making them up ...

In the afternoon she was finally able to observe Lídia and realized that she was as far from her as she was from the woman with the voice. They looked at one another and were unable to hate or even repel one another. Lídia spoke, pale and discreet, about several topics of no interest to either of them. Her burgeoning pregnancy floated about the room, filled it, penetrated Joana. Even the faded furniture, with the little crocheted doilies, seemed to conserve itself in the same almost-revealed secret, in the same expectancy of a child. Lídia's open eyes were shadowless. What a beautiful woman. Her full yet peaceful lips, without twitches, as if they belonged to someone who wasn't afraid of pleasure, who received it without remorse. On what poetry might her life be based? What might that murmuring she sensed inside Lídia be saying? The woman with the voice multiplied into countless women … But all said and done where was their divinity? Even in the weakest there was the shadow of the knowledge that is not acquired through intelligence. The intelligence of blind things. The power of a rock which when it topples bumps another that will fall into the sea and kill a fish. Sometimes the same power could be seen in women who were only slightly mothers and wives, men's timid females, like her aunt, like Armanda. Nevertheless that strength, unity in weakness … Oh, maybe she was exaggerating, maybe women's divinity wasn't specific, but merely resided in the fact of their existence. Yes, yes, there was the truth: they existed more than other people, they were the symbol of the thing in the thing itself. And woman was mystery in itself, she discovered. There was in all of them a quality of raw material, something that might one day define itself but which was never realized, because its real essence was "becoming." Wasn't it precisely through this that the past was united with the future and with all times?

Lídia and Joana fell silent for a long moment. They didn't feel exactly together, but without the need for words, as if they had actually only met to look at one another and then leave. The strangeness of the situation became clearer when the two of them felt that they weren't fighting. In both there was a movement of impatience, there was still a duty to fulfill. Joana pushed it away, suddenly satiated:

"Well," her own tone of voice woke her up unpleasantly, "I believe the interview is over."

Lídia was taken aback. But how? if they hadn't said anything! She was particularly put off by the idea of something unfinished:

"We haven't said anything yet … And we need to talk …"

Joana smiled. In this smile she began to act, not with force—weariness—but how exactly would I impress her. What nonsense am I thinking after all?

"Don't you feel," said Joana, "that we've gotten away from the reason that brought us together? If we talked about it, now at least, it would be without interest or passion … Let's leave it all for another day."

For an instant the figure of the man appeared to them lusterless, inopportune. But Lídia knew that no sooner had that woman disappeared, the inertia and stupor in which she had left her, taking away her desire to act, would also disappear. And awake again, she would want the child. The little family. She made an effort to come out of that sleepiness, to open her eyes and fight.

"It'd be absurd to miss this occasion …"

Yes, let's make the most of it, let's make the most of it. I feel listless because I prepared too much for the party. Joana laughed again, joylessly.

"I know I can't expect anything from you," continued pregnant Lídia suddenly with force—a cloud uncovering the sun, everything resplendent again, insufflated with life. Joana also lit up, felt the cloud uncovering the sun, everything bubbling lightly hand in hand in a soft circle, as if of children.

"I know you well," Lídia went on. Her words fell serenely dull into the lake, depositing themselves at the bottom, without consequence.

But suddenly she pushed herself and her pregnancy, in one last effort to wake up:

"I know you, I know how entrenched your evilness is."

Now the room came to life again.

"Oh, you do?"

Yes, it had come to life, thought Joana, waking up. What am I saying? How dare I come here? I am far, far away. All you have to do is look at this woman to see that one couldn't like me. The steel suddenly touched her heart. Ah, jealousy, it was jealousy, the cold hand mashing her slowly, squeezing her, diminishing her soul. With me the following either happens or threatens to happen: from one moment to the next, with a certain movement, I can make myself into a line. That's it! into a line of light, such that the person beside me ends up alone, unable to catch me and my deficiency. While Lídia has several planes. With each gesture another aspect of her dimension is revealed. Beside her no one slips and gets lost, because they support themselves on her breasts—serious, placid, pale, while mine are so futile—or on her belly where even a child fits. Don't exaggerate its importance, children can spring from all women's bellies. How lovely and womanly she is, serenely raw material, in spite of all other women. What is there in the air? I'm alone. Lídia's large lips, with unhurried lines, so well painted in pale lipstick, while my lipstick is dark, always scarlet, scarlet, scarlet, my face white and thin. Maybe those brown eyes of hers, enormous and tranquil, have nothing to give, but they receive so much that no one would be able to resist, much less Otávio. I'm a feathered creature, Lídia furry, Otávio gets lost between us, defenseless. How can he escape my shine and promise of flight and how can he escape this woman's certainty? The two of us could unite and supply humanity, we'd go from door to door early in the morning, ringing doorbells: which do you like: mine or hers? and we'd deliver a little child. I understand why Otávio didn't sever ties with Lídia: he is always willing to cast himself at the feet of those who walk forwards. He never sees a mountain without recognizing only its firmness, he never sees a woman with a large bust without thinking about laying his head on it. How poor I am compared to her, so self-assured. Either I light up and am wonderful, fleetingly wonderful, or I am obscure, wrapped in curtains. Lídia, whatever she is, is immutable, always with the same bright base. My hands and hers. Mine—sketched, solitary, lines shot forwards and backwards, carelessness and haste in a brush dipped in sad-white paint, I'm always raising my hand to my forehead, always threatening to leave them in the air, oh how futile I am, only now do I understand. Lídia's —clear-cut, pretty, covered in supple, rosy, yellowy skin, like a flower I saw somewhere, hands that rest on things, full of direction and wisdom. All of me swims, floats, crosses what exists with my nerves, I am nothing but a desire, anger, vagueness, as impalpable as energy. Energy? but where is my strength? in imprecision, in imprecision, in imprecision … And bringing life to it, not to reality, just the vague impulse forward. I want to awe Lídia, make the conversation something strange, fine, slipping away, but no, but yes, no, but why not? She suddenly remembered Otávio, stirring and blowing on his coffee mug to cool it, his expression serious, interested and naïve. Surprise Lídia, yes, drag her in … Like at that time at boarding school, when she suddenly needed to put her power to the test, to feel the admiration of her classmates, with whom she generally spoke little. So she performed coldly, making things up, shining as if exacting revenge. From the silence in which she hid, she came out to fight:

"Look at that man … He drinks white coffee in the morning, very slowly, dunking his bread in his mug, letting it drip, biting it, then getting up heavy, sad …"

Her classmates would look, see any man at all and yet, although surprised and intentionally distant at first, yet … it was miraculously exact! They would actually see the man getting up from the table … the empty mug … a few flies … Joana continued stalling for time, advancing, her eyes alight:

"And that other one … At night he takes his shoes off with an effort, tosses them aside, sighs, says: the important thing is not to lose heart, the important thing is not to lose heart …"

The weaker ones would murmur already smiling, dominated: it's true … how do you know? The others would hold back. But they'd end up surrounding Joana, waiting for her to show them something else. Her gestures by this time were light, febrile, and increasingly inspired she would touch them all:

"Look at that woman's eyes … round, transparent, trembling, trembling, out of the blue they might fall in a drop of water …"

"And what about that look?" Sometimes Joana was more audacious, finding sudden shyness in the girls who read certain books in the school corridors. "What about that look? of one who seeks pleasure wherever they can find it …"

Her classmates would laugh, but little by little something

slightly restless, painful and uncomfortable would creep into the scene. They'd end up laughing too much, nervous and dissatisfied. Joana, enthused, would rise above herself, holding the girls at her will and her word, full of a wit as stinging and sharp as light cracks of a whip. Until, finally drawn in, they were breathing her brilliant, suffocating air. In sudden satisfaction, Joana would then stop, her eyes dry, and body trembling over her victory. Slighted, feeling Joana's fast retreat and contempt, they would also droop wilted, as if embarrassed. One of them would say before they dispersed, tired of one another:

"Joana gets unbearable when she's cheerful …"

Lídia blushed. Joana's "Oh, you do?" had sounded so curt, distracted and curious, so far from Lídia's emotion.

"It doesn't matter, it doesn't matter," Joana tried to reassure her. "It's clear that you can't know what evilness is. So you're going to have a child …" she went on. "You want Otávio, the father. It's understandable. Why don't you get a job to support the kid? You were no doubt expecting great goodness from me, in spite of what you said just now about my evilness. But goodness really makes me want to be sick. Why don't you get a job? Then you wouldn't need Otávio. I'm not willing to grant you exactly everything. But first tell me about your affair with Otávio, tell me how you managed to get him to come back to you. Or better: what does he think of me. Don't be afraid to say it. Do I make him very unhappy?"

"I don't know, we don't mention your name."

So I was alone then? what about this happiness born of pain, the steel creasing my skin, this cold that is jealousy, no, this cold that is like this: oh, so you've come all this way? well you have to go back. But this time I won't start over, I swear, I won't rebuild anything, I'll stay behind like a rock off in the distance, at the beginning of the road. There is something that reels with me, reels, reels, dazes me, dazes me, and calmly deposits me back where I started.

She addressed Lídia:

"It's not possible ... He wouldn't set himself free so easily."

"But he detests you in a way!" Lídia shouted.

Well then.

"Do you sense that too?" Joana asked. "Yes, yes ... It isn't just hatred, in spite of everything." Last night, my tenderness, it doesn't matter, deep down I knew I was alone, I wasn't even fooled, because I knew, I knew. "What if it were fear too?"

"Fear? I don't understand," said Lídia, surprised. "Fear of what?"

"Maybe because I'm unhappy, fear of getting close. Maybe it's that: fear of having to suffer too ..."

"Are you unhappy?" Lídia asked in a quiet voice.

"But don't be afraid, unhappiness has nothing to do with evil," Joana laughed. — What happened after all? I'm not here, I'm not here, what happened, the weariness, I wish I could leave in tears. I know, I know: I'd like to spend at least one day watching Lídia walk from the kitchen to the living room, then eating lunch beside her in a quiet room (some flies, clinking cutlery), where no heat came in, wearing a big old floral robe. Later, in the afternoon, sitting and watching her sew, giving her a little hand here and there, the scissors, the thread, waiting for bath and dinner time, it'd be good, it'd be expansive and fresh. Could it be that I've always been lacking a little of this? Why is she so powerful? The fact that I've never had afternoons of sewing doesn't place me beneath her, I suppose. Or does it? It does, it doesn't, it does, it doesn't. I know what I want: an ugly, clean woman with large breasts, who tells me: what's all this about making things up? I won't have any dramas, come here immediately!—And she gives me a warm bath, dresses me in a white linen nightdress, braids my hair and puts me to bed, very cross, saying: well what do you want? you run wild, eating at odd times, you could get sick, stop making up tragedies, you think you're such a big deal, drink this mug of hot broth. She lifts my head up with her hand, covers me with a big sheet, brushes a few strands of hair off my forehead, already white and fresh, and tells me before I fall asleep warmly: you'll see how in no time your face is going to fill out, forget those harebrained ideas and be a good girl. Someone who takes me in like a humble dog, who opens the door for me, brushes me, feeds me, loves me severely like a dog, that's all I want, like a dog, a child.

"Would you like to be married—really married—to him?" asked Joana.

Lídia glanced at her, trying to work out if there was any sarcasm in her question:

"I would."

"Why?" asked Joana in surprise. "Don't you see there's nothing to gain with it? Everything there is in marriage you already have." Lídia blushed, but I wasn't being mean, ugly, clean woman. "I bet you spent your whole life wanting to get married." Lídia had a moment of revolt: she'd been touched right in her wound, coldly.

"Yes. Every woman …" she concurred.

"Not in my case. Because I never thought about getting married. The funny thing is I'm still sure I'm not married … I believed more or less this: marriage is the end, after marrying nothing else can happen to me. Imagine: always having someone beside you, never knowing solitude.—Good God!—not being with myself ever, ever. And being a married woman, that is, a person with her destiny all mapped out. From then on all you do is wait to die. I thought: not even the freedom to be unhappy is preserved because you are dragging another person around with you. There is someone who is always observing you, who scrutinizes you, who sees your every move. And even the weariness of living has a certain beauty when it is born alone and desperate—I thought. But as a couple, eating the same bland bread every day, watching your own defeat in the other person's defeat … All this without considering the weight of your habits reflected in the other person's habits, the weight of the common bed, the common table, the common life, preparing and threatening the common death. I always said: never."

"Why did you marry?" asked Lídia.

"I don't know. All I know is that this 'I don't know' doesn't mean I don't know in this particular case, rather it is the backdrop for things." I'm straying from the topic, soon she'll give me that look that I know all too well. "I got married no doubt because I wanted to get married. Because Otávio wanted to marry me. That's it, that's it: I've worked it out: instead of asking to live with me without marriage, he suggested something else. In fact it wouldn't have made any difference. And I was besotted, Otávio is handsome, isn't he? I didn't think about anything else." Pause. "How is it that you want him: with your body?"

"Yes, with my body," Lídia had stammered.

"It's love."

"What about you?" dared Lídia.

"Not so much."

"But he told me, on the contrary …"

Lídia stopped short. She studied her carefully. How inexperienced Joana seemed. She spoke of love with such simplicity and clarity because doubtless nothing had been revealed to her through it yet. She hadn't fallen into its shadows, she still hadn't felt its profound and secret transformations. Otherwise she'd be, like herself, almost ashamed of so much happiness, she'd stay vigilant at its door, protecting from the cold light that which couldn't be scorched in order to stay alive. Nevertheless that vivacity of Joana's … which she had understood through Otávio … that there was life inside her … But her love offered no shelter, not even for Joana herself, sensed Lídia. Inexperienced, upright, untouched, she could be mistaken for a virgin. Lídia gazed at her and tried to explain to herself what was so oscillating and lucid in that face. Unquestionably love didn't connect her even to love. While she herself, Lídia, almost an instant after the first kiss, had become a woman.

"Yes, yes, but it doesn't change anything," continued Joana serenely. "I also want him more coldly, as an animal, as a man." I wonder if she's going to look at me in that fearful, astounded, reverent manner: oh, because you talk about difficult things, because you come out with enormous things at simple moments, spare me, spare me. But this time it's my fault, because I really don't know what I meant to say. However it is like this that I will beat her.

Lídia hesitated:

"Isn't that more than love?"

"Maybe," said Joana surprised. "What matters is that it is no longer love." And suddenly along comes the weariness, the big "so that" drawing me in, and I know I'm going to say something. "Keep Otávio. Have his child, be happy and leave me be."

"Do you know what you're saying?" Lídia cried.

"Yes, of course."

"You don't like him …"

"I do. But I've never known what to do with the people and

the things I like, sometimes they weigh me down, ever since I was a girl. Maybe if I really liked him with my body … Maybe I'd care more …" These are confidences, good God. Now I'm going to say: "Otávio runs from me because I don't bring anyone peace, I am always the same millstone to others, I make them say: I was blind, it wasn't peace that I had, and now I want it."

"Even so … I think … no one can complain … Not even Otávio … not even me I suppose …" Lídia was unable to explain, she'd grown vague, her hands didn't rest on things.

"What?"

"I don't know." She looked at Joana and sought something in her face, intrigued, moving her head.

"What is it?" repeated Joana.

"I can't understand."

Joana blushed slightly:

"Neither can I. I've never delved into my heart."

Something had been said.

Joana walked over to the window, looked at the garden where Lídia's child would play, the child that was now in Lídia's belly, that would be fed by Lídia's breasts, that would be Lídia. Or Otávio, unripe fruit? No, Lídia, the one who transmits herself. If someone were to split her in half—the sound of fresh leaves breaking—they would see her as an open pomegranate, healthy and pink, translucent with clear eyes. The base of her life was as docile as a brook running through the countryside. And in this countryside she herself moved as confident and serene as an animal grazing. She compared her to Otávio, for whom life would never be more than a narrow individual adventure. And with herself, using others as a dark backdrop against which her tall, brilliant figure stood in silhouette. Lídia's poetry: only this silence is my prayer, Lord, and I don't know what else to say; I am so happy to feel that I stay quiet in order to feel more; it was in silence that a light, tender spider web was born in me: this soft incomprehension of life that allows me to live. Or was it all a lie? Oh, God, when she most needed to take action she lost herself in useless thoughts. All no doubt a lie, it was even possible that Lídia was much less pure than she imagined. But even so she was reticent to remain by her side, accidentally look at her a little forcefully, make her aware of herself. Preserve her, don't transform her color, her precious voice.

"He told me about what happened with the old man ... You threw the book at him, so old ... Before I understood, but now I don't know how you could ..." Lídia asked.

"But it was true."

Lídia stared at her, lips slightly open, waiting for her. And suddenly she felt with clarity that she didn't want to fight that woman. She shook her head disoriented. Her face dissolved, shook, her features hesitated in search of an expression:

"I didn't do it on purpose, you know? No, I didn't ..." Lídia remained restless, her face stung by quick twitches. "Why would I want to fool you? No, that's not what I mean, that's not it ..."

And suddenly, without Joana expecting it, she burst into free, loud sobbing. She's with child, she's upset, thought Joana. Lídia was dragging arduously:

"I wouldn't mind taking Otávio from another woman. But I didn't know that there was you ... Not just anybody, like me but someone so ... so good ... so sublime ..."

Joana was startled. Ah, I was striving for that: I've managed to be sublime ... like in the old days ... No, it's not entirely like that, I didn't force the situation, how could I with this steel creasing and chilling my body? Don't put myself in this light, with the furrow in my forehead so evident. Seek that degree of light and shadow in which I suddenly become fleshy, my lipstick darkened in an old streak of blood, my face white under my hair ... The steel blade presses against my heart again. When I leave she'll despise me only as long as she is in awe. I am fleetingly wonderful ... God, God ... I walk running, delirious, my body flying, hesitating ... where to? There is a frightened, light substance in the air, I have managed to obtain it, it is like the instant that precedes a child's crying. That night, I don't know when, there were staircases, fans moving, tender lights shaking their sweet rays like the heads of tolerant mothers, there was a man looking at me from over on the line of the horizon, I was a stranger, but I won anyway, even if it was slighting something. Everything slid softly, in silent combination. It was towards the end—end of what? of the noble and languid staircase, sloping, waving its long shiny arm, the beautiful, proud handrail, the end of the night—when I was gliding into the centre of the room, as soft as an air bubble. And suddenly, strong as thunder but silent as a silent fright, and, suddenly, another step and I couldn't continue! The hem of my chiffon dress quivered in a grimace, struggled, twisted, tore on the sharp corner of a piece of furniture and remained there, tremulous, panting, perplexed under my dumbfounded gaze. And suddenly things had hardened, an orchestra had burst into crooked sounds and silenced immediately, there was something triumphant and tragic in the air. I discovered that deep down there was no surprise in me: that everything was heading slowly towards this and had now catapulted into its true plane. I wanted to run away, crying with my poor dress, hemless, torn and distressed. Now the lights were shining with force and pride, the fans unveiling resplendent, astute faces, from far off on the horizon the man was smiling at me, the handrail drew back, closed its eyes ... No one needed to lie anymore, since I already knew everything! Now I shall leap into another state too. Why? Why? I'm leaving here, I'm going home, all of a sudden the tear in my dress, hear the orchestra's piercing scream and suddenly the silence, all of the musicians lying dead on the platform, in the big hall, angry and empty. Look the tear in the face, but I've always been afraid of bursting with suffering, like the orchestra's scream. No one knows to what extent I can arrive almost in triumph as if I were a creation: it is a feeling of extra-human power attained at a certain degree of suffering. One minute more however and you don't know if it's power or absolute impotence, just like wanting with your body and your brain to move a finger and simply not being able to. It's not simply not being able to: but all things laughing and crying at the same time. No, I certainly didn't invent this situation, and that's what surprises me the most. Because my desire for experience wouldn't go as far as to provoke this cold iron pressing against warm flesh, finally warm from yesterday's tenderness. Oh, don't martyr yourself: you know that you wouldn't remain in the same state for long: you would again open and close circles of life, tossing them aside, withered ... That moment would also pass, even if Lídia didn't demand Otávio, even if I never found out that Otávio hadn't left her although he was married to me. Am I not mixing into this threat of pain a certain sweet, ironic happiness? Am I not loving myself at this moment? Only when I leave here will I allow myself to look at the tear in my dress. Nothing happened, except that yesterday I had begun a renewal and now I am withdrawing because this woman is upset because she is expecting Otávio's child. First and foremost there has been no essential transformation, all this already existed, there was just the tear in the dress indicating things. And really, really, headache, tiredness, really everything was heading for this.

"I can have a child too," she said aloud. Her voice sounded beautiful and limpid.

"Yes," Lídia murmured in dismay.

"I can too. Why not?"

"No …"

"No? But yes … I'll give you Otávio, not now, but when I want to. I'll have a child and then I'll give Otávio back to you."

"But that is monstrous!" Lídia shouted.

"But why? Is it monstrous to have two women? You know very well it isn't. It's nice being pregnant, I imagine. But is it enough for someone to be expecting a child or is it still too little?"

"It feels good," Lídia said dragged in, her eyes open.

"Good?"

"You also dread the birth sometimes," answered Lídia mechanically.

"Don't be afraid, any animal can have young. You'll have an easy birth and so will I. We both have wide hips."

"Yes …"

"I also want the things life has to offer. Why not? Do you think I'm sterile? Not at all. I haven't had children because I didn't want to."

I can feel myself holding a child, thought Joana. Sleep, my child, sleep, I tell you. The child is warm and I am sad. But it is the sadness of happiness, this appeasement and sufficiency that leave the face placid, faraway. And when my child touches me he doesn't rob me of my thoughts as others do. But later, when I give him milk with these fragile, beautiful breasts, my child will grow from my force and crush me with his life. He will distance himself from me and I will be the useless old mother. I won't feel cheated. But defeated merely and I will say: I don't know a thing, I am able to give birth to a child and I don't know a thing. God will receive my humility and will say: I was able to give birth to a world and I don't know a thing. I will be closer to Him and to the woman with the voice. My child will move in my arms and I will tell myself: Joana, Joana this is good. I won't utter another word because the truth will be what pleases my arms.

The Man

BETWEEN ONE INSTANT AND ANOTHER, BETWEEN past and future, the white vagueness of the interval. Empty like the distance from one minute to the next in the clock's circle. The bottom of events rising up silent and dead, a little bit of eternity.

Just a quiet second perhaps separating one stretch of life from the next. Not even a second, she couldn't count it in time, but long like an infinite straight line. Deep, coming from far off—a black bird, a dot growing on the horizon, drawing closer to awareness like a ball thrown from the end to the beginning. And exploding before perplexed eyes in an essence of silence. Leaving behind it the perfect interval like a single sound vibrating in the air. Be reborn later, store away the strange memory of the interval, not knowing how to mix it into life. Carry forever the small empty dot—dazed and virgin, too fleeting to allow itself to be revealed.

Joana felt it as she crossed Lídia's small garden, ignorant as to where she was going, knowing only that she was leaving behind her everything she had ever experienced. When she closed the little gate, she distanced herself from Lídia, from Otávio, and, alone in herself again, she walked.

The beginning of a storm had settled and the cool air circulated softly. She climbed the hill again and her heart still beat without rhythm. She sought the peace of those paths at that hour, between the afternoon and the night, an invisible cicada whispering the same song. The moist old walls in ruins, invaded by ivy and creepers sensitive to the wind. She stopped and without her footsteps she heard the silence moving. Only her body disturbed the serenity. She imagined it without her presence and sensed the freshness that those dead things mixed with others must have, fragilely alive like at the beginning of creation.

The tall closed houses, withdrawn like towers. Access to one of the mansions was via a long, shadowy, quiet street, the end of the world. It was only next to it that a slope could be seen, the birth of another street and one realized that it wasn't the end. The low, broad mansion, the broken windows, the closed venetians, covered in dust. She was very familiar with that garden where soft tufts of weed, red roses, rusted old cans mingled. Under the flowering jasmine vines she would find faded newspapers, pieces of moist wood from old grafts. Among the heavy, aged trees sparrows and pigeons had been pecking at the ground forever. A little bird was resting from flight, strolling around the environs until it disappeared into a thicket. The proud sweet mansion in its debris. To die there. One could only arrive at that house when the end came. To die on that moist earth so good for receiving a dead body. But it wasn't death that she wanted, she was afraid too.

A trickle of water ran unceasingly down the dark wall. Joana stopped for a moment, stared at it empty, impassive. On one of her walks she had sat next to the rusty little gate, her face pressed against the cold bars, trying to sink into the moist, dark smell of the yard. That cloistered quietness, the perfume. But that had been a long time ago. Now she had cut herself off from the past.

She kept walking. She no longer felt the heat of the fever that the conversation with Lídia had brought on. She was pallid and her excess tiredness was now making her almost light, her features finer, purified. Again she hoped for an end, the end that never came to complete her moments. She wished something inevitable would descend over her, she wanted to cede, to submit. At times her steps took the wrong direction, they felt heavy, her legs barely moved. But she pushed herself, saving herself to fall further away. She looked at the ground, the blonde grasses that were humbly reborn after each crushing.

She raised her eyes and saw him. That same man who followed her frequently, without ever approaching her. She had already seen him many times in those same streets, on her afternoon walk. She wasn't surprised. Something would have to come somehow, she knew. Sharp as a knife. Yes, just the night before, lying next to Otávio, unaware of what would come to pass the next day, she had remembered this man. Sharp as a knife ... Feeling slightly dizzy, as she tried to make him out from a distance, she saw him multiply into innumerous figures that filled the path tremulous and formless. When the darkness left her vision, her forehead moist with sweat, she saw him in contrast as a poor, single dot walking towards her, lost on the long, deserted street. He would no doubt just follow her, as he had the other times. But she was tired and stopped.

The figure of the man drew closer and closer and grew, Joana felt she was sinking deeper and deeper into the irremediable.

She could still retreat, she could still turn her back and leave, avoiding him. It wouldn't even be running away, she sensed the man's humility. Nothing held her there immobile clearly waiting for him to approach her. Nothing held her, not even fear. But even if death was drawing near now, even vileness, hope or pain again. She had simply stopped. The veins that connected her to the things she had experienced had been cut, gathered up in a single faraway block, demanding a logical continuation, but old, dead. Only she herself had survived, still breathing. And in front of her a new field, still colorless, the dawn emerging. Cross its mists to see it. She couldn't turn back, she didn't know why she should turn back. If she still hesitated before the stranger drawing closer and closer it was because she feared the life that was again approaching relentless. She tried to cling to the interval, to exist in it suspended, in that cold, abstract world, without mixing with the blood.

He came. He stopped a few steps away from her. They remained silent. She with wide, staring, tired eyes. He shaky, hesitant. Around them the leaves moved in the breeze, a bird cheeped monotonously.

The silence stretched out waiting for what they might say. But neither of them discovered in the other the beginning of a word. They both melted into quietness. He slowly stopped palpitating, his eyes rested more deeply in Joana's body, softly took possession of it and its weariness. He stared at her forgetting himself and his shyness. Joana felt him penetrate her and let him.

When he spoke she raised her body imperceptibly. It felt like a very long time had passed, but when he uttered his first words without attempting to start a conversation she knew that she had in fact distanced herself incommensurably from the beginning.

"I live in that house," he said.

She waited.

"Do you want to rest?"

Joana nodded and he looked mutely at the luminous aura that her unkempt hair drew around her small head. He went ahead and she followed him.

When he spoke she raised her body imperceptibly, he pulled down the curtains and shadow spread across the wooden floor, to the closed door. He pulled up a soft, old armchair for her, and she sank into it, her legs tucked up. He himself sat on the edge of the narrow bed, covered with a crumpled sheet. He sat there unmoving, hands together, looking at her.

Joana closed her eyes. She heard soft noises stretch distantly through the house, a child's exclamation of mild surprise. As if from another world, the fresh cry of a faraway rooster sounded. Behind everything, light water running, the wheezing, rhythmic breathing of the trees.

A movement sensed nearby made her open her eyes. She didn't notice him at first, in the half-darkness of the room. She made him out little by little kneeling by the bed, his face wavering in his hands. She wanted to call him and didn't know how. She didn't want to touch him. However the man's anguish came to her more and more and Joana moved on the armchair, waiting for his look.

He raised his head and Joana was surprised. The man's parted lips shone moist as if a light were illuminating him on the inside. His eyes shone, but she couldn't tell if from pain or mysterious cheer. His forehead had expanded upwards, his body could barely keep its balance in the effort to contain itself, to not vibrate.

"What?" whispered Joana fascinated.

He looked at her.

"I'm afraid," he said finally.

They stared at one another for a second. And she wasn't afraid, but felt a compact happiness, more intense than terror, take possession of her and fill her entire body.

"I'll return to this house," she said.

He faced her suddenly terrified, without breathing. For an instant she expected him to shout or invent a crazy movement that she couldn't even begin to guess. The man's lips trembled a moment. And barely freeing himself from Joana's gaze, fleeing it like a madman, he brusquely hid his face in his long, thin hands.

Refuge in the Man

JOANA, JOANA, THOUGHT THE MAN AS HE WAITED FOR her to arrive. Joana, naked name, saintly Joana, so virginal. How pure and innocent she was. He saw her childlike features, her hands as eloquent as a blind man's. She wasn't pretty, at least in his manhood he'd never dreamed of that creature, never desired her. Perhaps that was why he'd followed her through the streets so many times, even though he hadn't expected her to look at him, perhaps ... He wasn't sure, he'd always liked seeing her. She wasn't pretty. Or was she? How could he tell? It was so hard to figure out as if he'd never seen her before, as if he hadn't embraced her so many times. A threat of transformation on her face, in her movements, instant by instant. Even resting she was something that was about to rise. And what did he understand now and feel so miraculously, as if she had explained it to him?—he asked himself. He closed his eyes, his arms next to him on the bed. But only until Joana's footsteps could be heard outside. Because he never dared let himself go in her presence. He leaned over her, waited for her every second, absorbing her. He never tired, however, and the posture didn't take away his naturalness. It just thrust him into another kind hitherto unknown. He was two, now, but his new emergent being slowly grew and dominated the past of the other. He pressed his lips together. He felt that mysteriously there was logic in his having experienced certain kinds of torture, serene abjection, his unconcerned lack of direction, to now receive Joana at long last. Not that anyone had ever pushed him into the mud or against his will, not that he considered himself a martyr. He had never expected a solution. Even as regarded women, whom he watched, watched and abandoned. Even the woman in whose house he had now lazily installed himself, although he could barely stand her presence, a tiresome, tender shadow. He had walked on his own two feet, his body aware, experimenting and suffering without tenderness toward himself, coldly, naively granting his curiosity everything. He had even believed he was happy. And now Joana had come along, she, Joana who … He wanted to add another word, the true one, the difficult one, to his confused thoughts, but he was assailed again by the idea that he didn't need to think any more, he didn't need anything, anything … she'd arrive soon. Soon. But listen: soon … That was it: Joana had freed him. More and more he needed less in order to live: he thought less, ate less, barely slept at all. She was always. And she'd arrive soon.

He closed his eyes more intensely, bit his lips, suffering without knowing why. He immediately opened them again and in the room—the empty room!—he suddenly couldn't find proof that Joana had been there. As if her existence were a lie … He got up. Come, shouted something burning and mortal in him. Come, he repeated in a low voice, full of fear, his gaze lost. Come …

Almost silent footsteps trod through the dry leaves outside.

Joana was arriving again ... again she heard him from a distance.

He stood next to the bed, his eyes absent, a blind man listening to distant music. She drew closer, closer ... Joana. Her footsteps were more and more a reality, the only reality. Joana. With the abruptness of a stab, pain burst in his body, lighting him up with happiness and perplexity.

When the door opened for Joana he ceased to exist. He slid deep down inside himself, hovering in the penumbra of his own unsuspecting forest. He moved a little now and his gestures were easy and new. His pupils dark and wide, suddenly a slight animal, frightened as a deer. Meanwhile the atmosphere had become so lucid that he would have noticed any movement by any living thing in his vicinity. And his body was nothing but fresh memory, where sensations would be molded as if for the first time.

The small white ship floated on thick waves, green, bright and shoddy—he saw her lying there, staring at the little picture on the wall.

"On the 3rd," continued Joana making her voice clear, light, with small round intervals, "on the 3rd there was a big parade for those who were being born. It was so funny to see the people singing and holding flags full of every non-color. Then a man as tenuous and swift as the breeze that blows when you're sad got up and said from afar: me. No one heard him, but he was almost satisfied. That was when the great gale that blows from the northwest rose up and stomped on everyone with its big fiery feet. They all went home, withered, scorched from the heat. They took off their shoes, loosened their collars. All bloods ran slowly, heavily in all veins. And a big not-having-anything-to-do dragged through people's souls. In the interim the earth kept turning. That was when a boy called a name was born. He was beautiful, the boy. Big eyes that saw, delicate lips that felt, narrow face that felt, high forehead that felt. His head was large. He walked like someone who knew the place exactly, slipping effortlessly through the crowd. Whoever followed him would arrive. When he was moved, when he was surprised, he'd shake his head, like this, slowly, like someone receiving more than he'd expected. He was beautiful. And above all he was alive. And above all I loved him. I was born, and my heart was new whenever I saw him. I was born, I was born, I was born. Now a verse. What I want, my dear, is to see you always, my dear. Like I saw you today, my dear. Even if you die, my dear. Another one: one day I heard a flower singing and calmly rejoiced; then I walked over and, miraculously, it wasn't the flower that was singing but a little bird above the flower."

Joana was speaking sleepily by the end. Through her half-closed eyes the ship was floating crooked in the painting, things in the room were stretching out, glowing, the end of one holding hands with the start of another. Because if she already knew "that everything was one," why continue seeing and living? The man, with his eyes closed, had sunk into her shoulder and listened dreaming without sleeping. Every so often she heard in the keen silence of the summer afternoon slow, muffled movements on the loose wooden floor. It was the woman, the woman, that woman.

The first few times Joana had come to the big house, she had wanted to ask the man this: is she like your mother now? she's not your lover any more? she still wants you in the house even though I exist? But she had always put it off. However, the other woman's presence in the house was so great, that the three of them formed a pair. And Joana and the man never felt entirely alone. Joana had also wanted to ask the woman herself:

but where, but where does your soul unravel behind you? That however was an old thought. Because one day she had seen her out of the corner of her eye, her fat back concentrated into an indissoluble block of anguish under her black lace dress. She had also noticed her at other, fleeting, moments, going from a bedroom to the living room, smiling quickly, escaping horrible. Then Joana had discovered that she was someone alive and dark. Thick ears, sad and heavy, with a black cave in the middle. The tender, fugitive and cheerful gaze of a prostitute without glory. The moist lips, wilted, large, heavily made up. How she must love the man. Her fluffy hair was thinning and reddish from repeated dyeing. And the room where the man slept and received Joana, that room with the curtains, almost dustless, she had tidied no doubt. Like a woman sewing her son's shroud. Joana, that woman and the teacher's wife. What connected them after all? The three diabolical graces.

"Almonds …" said Joana, turning to the man. "The mystery and the sweetness of words: almond … listen, pronounced carefully, voice in my throat, echoing in the depths of my mouth. It vibrates, leaves me long and drawn out and curved like an arch. Bitter, poisonous and pure almond."

The three bitter, poisonous and pure graces.

"Tell me that one …" said the man.

"What one?"

"About the sailor. If you love a sailor you'll have loved the whole world."

"Horrible …" laughed Joana. "I know: I said myself that it must be so true that it was born rhyming. But I don't remember it any more."

"It was Sunday in the square. The quay in the port …" the man prompted.

One day, breaking his usual quietness around Joana he had tried to speak:

"I've always never been anything."

"Yes," she replied.

"But everything that has happened wouldn't make you leave …"

"No."

"Even this woman … this house … It's different, you know?"

"I know."

"I've always been like a beggar, I know. But I've never asked for, or needed, or known anything. You came, you know? I used to think: nothing was bad. But now … Why do you always tell me such crazy things, I swear, I can't …"

She had then propped herself up on her elbow, suddenly serious, her face leaning over him:

"Do you believe me?"

"Yes …" he had answered surprised by her violence.

"You know that I don't lie, that I never lie, even when … even always? Do you feel it? say it, say it. The rest doesn't matter then, nothing would matter … When I say these things … these crazy things, when I don't want to know about your past and I don't want to tell you about me, when I make up words … When I lie do you feel that I'm not lying?"

"Yes, yes …"

She had flopped back onto the bed, eyes closed, tired. It doesn't matter, it doesn't matter if later he doesn't believe me, if he runs from me like the teacher. For now when she was with him she could think. And for now is time too. She opened her eyes, smiled at him. A boy, that's what he is. He must have had many women, very loved, attractive, with his long eyelashes, his cold eyes. Until now he was more consistent, I've dissolved him a little. That woman hopes that one day I'll finally leave. That he'll return.

"It was Sunday in the square? The square is wide and solitary," she said finally slowly trying to remember and fulfill the man's request. "Yes … So much sun, stuck to the ground as if it was born of it. The sea, the belly of the sea, silent, laboring for breath. The fish in Sunday, swiftly waving their tails and serenely continuing to forge ahead. A still ship. Sunday. The sailors strolling along the quay, through the square. A pink dress appearing and disappearing on a street corner. The trees crystallized in Sunday (Sunday is something like Christmas trees), shining silent, holding, like this, like this, their breath. A man going past with a woman in a new dress. The man wants to not be anything, he walks beside her looking at her almost face-on, asking her, asking her: speak, demand, walk. Her not answering, smiling, pure Sunday. Satisfaction, satisfaction. Pure sadness without hurt. Sadness that seems to come from behind the woman in pink. Sunday sadness on the quay in the port, the sailors lent to the earth. This light sadness is the realization of living. Since no one knows how to use this sudden knowledge, sadness comes."

"This time the story was different," he complained after a pause.

"It's just that I'm only saying what I saw and not what I see. I don't know how to repeat, I only know things once," she explained to him.

"It was different, but everything that you see is perfect."

Around his neck he wore a little chain with a small gold medallion. On one side Saint Thérèse, on the other Saint Christopher. He was a devotee of both:

"But I'm not really interested in saints. Just sometimes."

She had once told him that when she was a child she could spend a whole afternoon playing with a word. So he asked her to invent new ones. She had never wanted him as much as she did at those moments.

"Tell me again what Lalande is," he begged Joana.

"It's like angel's tears. Do you know what angel's tears is? A kind of little narcissus, the slightest breeze will make it bend this way and that. Lalande is also the night sea, when no one has set eyes on the beach yet, when the sun hasn't risen. Every time I say: Lalande, you should feel the cool, salty sea breeze, you should walk along the still-dark beach, slowly, naked. Soon you will feel Lalande ... Believe me, I'm one of the people who knows the sea best.

He didn't know at times if he was alive or if he was dead, if everything he had was too little or too much. When she spoke, she invented crazy, crazy! Plenitude filled him up as big as an empty space and his torment was that of the clarity of the wide space above the waters. Why was he always dumbstruck in her presence, dazed like a white wall in the moonlight? Or perhaps he'd wake up suddenly and shout: who is this woman? she is too much in my life! I can't ... I want to go back ... But he couldn't any more—he felt suddenly with a fright, lost.

"Darling," she said interrupting the man's thoughts.

"Yes, yes ..." He hid his face in that soft shoulder and she felt his breathing travel through her back and forth, back and forth. They were two living beings. What else matters? she thought. He moved, positioned his head on her flesh like ... like an amoeba, a protozoan blindly seeking the nucleus, the live center. Or like a child. Outside the world slid past, and the day, the day, then the night, then the day. Some time she would have to leave, to separate again. So would he. From her?

Yes, soon she would become too heavy for him with her excess of miracle. Like everyone else, inexplicably ashamed of himself he would long to leave. But revenge: he wouldn't free himself entirely. He'd end up in awe of himself, committing himself, full of an undefined, agonizing responsibility. Joana smiled. He would end up hating her, as if she were demanding something of him. Like her aunt and uncle who respected her however, sensing that she didn't love her pleasures. Confusedly they supposed her to be superior and despised her. Oh God, she was remembering again, telling herself her story, justifying herself … She could ask the man for facts: is that what I'm like? But what did he know? He leaned his face into her shoulder, hid, possibly happy at that moment. Shake him, tell him; man, that's what Joana was like, man. And with that she became a woman and aged. She believed herself to be very powerful and felt unhappy. So powerful that she imagined she had chosen her paths before she had traveled them—and only in thought. So unhappy that, judging herself powerful, she didn't know what to do with her power and saw each minute lost because she hadn't guided it to an end. That was how Joana grew, man, slender as a pine tree, very courageous too. Her courage had developed in the bedroom and with the light off glowing worlds formed without fear and without modesty. She learned to think at a young age and because she hadn't seen any human being up close except herself, she was awe-struck, she suffered, her pride was painful, sometimes light but almost always difficult to carry. How to end Joana's story? If she could take the look she had caught on Lídia and add it: no one will love you … Yes, end like that: even though she was one of those creatures that are straggling and alone in the world, no one had ever thought to give Joana anything. Not love, they always gave her some other emotion. She lived her life, avid as a virgin—and would be to the grave. She asked herself many questions, but she could never answer herself: she'd stop in order to feel. How was a triangle born? as an idea first? or did it come after the shape had been executed? would a triangle be born fatally? things were rich.—She would want to spend time on the question. But love invaded her. Triangle, circle, straight lines ... as harmonious and mysterious as an arpeggio. Where does music go when it's not playing?—she asked herself. And disarmed she would answer: may they make a harp out of my nerves when I die.

The end of Joana's lucidity mixed with the crooked ship on the waves, moving? moving. All she had to do was waggle her head for the waves to accompany it. But she had had things, ah had she ever. A husband, breasts, a lover, a house, books, short hair, an aunt, a teacher. Aunty, listen to me, I knew Joana, of whom I speak now. She was a weak woman with regards to things. Everything struck her at times as too precious, impossible to touch. And, at times, what people used as air to breathe, was weight and death for her. Try to understand my heroine, Aunty, listen. She is vague and audacious. She doesn't love, she isn't loved. You would end up noticing it as Lídia, another woman (a young woman full of her own destiny), observed it. However what Joana has inside her is something stronger than the love that people give and what she has inside her demands more than the love that people receive. Do you understand, Aunty? I wouldn't call her a hero, as I promised Daddy myself. Because in her there was a great fear. A fear prior to any judgment and understanding.—This occurred to me just now: maybe, just maybe belief in future survival comes when you realize that life always leaves us untouched.—Do you understand, Aunty? — forget the interruption of future life — do you understand? I see your eyes open, looking at me with fear, with distrust, but wanting even so, with your old woman's femininity, now dead, it is true, now dead, to like me, overlooking my asperity. Poor dear! The biggest indignation that I felt in you, besides that which I provoked, can be summed up in the almost daily sentence that I still hear, mixed with your smell that I can't forget: "oh, not being able to go out in the clothes you are wearing!" What else can I tell you? My hair is short, brown, sometimes I wear a fringe. I am going to die one day. I was born too. There was the room with the two of them. He was handsome. The room spun a little. It would become transparent and warm a veil a veil drawing closer coming. The three of them formed a couple and who could she tell it to? She was able to sleep because the man never slept and would keep watch like the rain falling. Otávio was handsome too, eyes. The man was a child an amoeba flowers whiteness warmth like sleep for now is time for now is life even if it is later ... Everything like the land a child Lídia a child Otávio land de profundis ...

The Viper

THAT I SOFTLY OVERCOME SOMETHING ...

Otávio was reading as the clock clacked the seconds and rended the silence of the night with 11 chimes.

That I softly overcome something ... That's what it seems like. This lightness is coming from I don't know where. Curtains drape over their own waists languidly. But also the black stain, unmoving, two eyes staring and not being able to say a thing. God perches in a tree chirping and straight lines travel on unfinished, horizontal and cold. That's what it seems like ... The moments keep dripping ripe and no sooner has one tumbled than another rises up, somewhat, its face pale and tiny. Suddenly the moments end too. Timelessness trickles through my walls, tortuous and blind. It slowly collects in a dark, quiet pool and I shout: I've lived!

The night silenced things outside, a toad croaked every now and then. Each bush was an unmoving, withdrawn mass.

Far off little reddish lights twinkled and shook, unsleeping eyes. In the darkness like the water's.

The tall, thin sunflowers lit up the garden in pauses.

What to think at that instant? She was so pure and free that she could choose and didn't know it. She could make something out, but wouldn't have been able to say it or think it at all, so diluted was the image in the darkness of her body. She just felt it and looked expectantly through the window as if at her own face in the night. Was this the most she would attain? To get close, close, almost touch it, but feel the wave behind her sucking her back in a firm, soft ebb, drinking her, leaving her afterwards with the haunting, impalpable memory of a hallucination … Even at that moment, perceiving the night and her own indistinct thoughts, she still remained separate to them, always a small closed block, watching, watching. The little light twinkling silently, set apart, solitary, unconquered. She never surrendered herself.

She looked around, the sitting room panting a little, weakly lit as if in a swoon. She lifted her head slightly, examined the space and was aware of the rest of the house that was lost in the darkness, serious and vague objects floating through corners. She would have to feel her way as soon as she was through the door. And especially if she were a child, in her aunt's house, waking up at night, mouth dry, going to look for water. Knowing the people were each isolated inside their impenetrable, secret sleep. Especially if she were that child and like on that night or those nights, as she crossed the kitchen she came upon the moonlight motionless in the yard like in a cemetery, the free, indecisive wind … Especially if she were the frightened child she would bump into imprecise objects in the dark and with each touch they would suddenly condense into chairs and tables, into barriers, with open, cold, intransigent eyes. But also imprisoned then. After the thump the pain, the moonlight exposing the cement terrace, thirst rising up through her body like a memory. The profound quiet of the house, the motionless, livid neighboring rooftops …

Again Joana tried to return to the sitting room, to Otávio's presence. She was detached from things, from her own things, created by herself and alive. She could be left in the desert, in the solitude of the glaciers, any place on Earth and she would still have the same white, fallen hands, the same almost serene disconnectedness. Take a bundle of clothes, leave slowly. Don't run away, but go. That's it, so sweet: don't run away, but go … Or shout out loud, loud and straight and infinite, with closed, calm eyes. Walk until I find the little red lights. As shaky as at a beginning or an end. Was she also dying or being born? No, don't go: stay bound to the moment just as a rapt gaze clings to the vacuum, quiet, stationary in the air …

The rattling of a faraway streetcar passed through her as if in a tunnel. A night train in a tunnel. Farewell. No, those who travel at night just look through the window and don't say farewell. No one knows where the hovels are, the dirty bodies are dark and don't require light.

"Otávio," she said because she was lost.

Joana's voice grazed the inexpressive room, light, direct. He raised his eyes:

"What is it?" he asked. And his voice was full of blood and flesh, it reunited the room in the room, designated and defined things. A breath of air fanning the flames. The crowd had entered the empty square.

She thrashed about for a moment, shook, woke up. Everything shone again in the lamplight, as calm and cheerful as if in a home. Within the penumbra of her body the uselessness of waiting passed through her sleepwalking like a bird through the night.

"Otávio," she repeated.

He was waiting. Then aware of the room, the man and herself once again, her own flames grew a little, she knew that she should proceed logically, that the man was waiting for a continuation. She sought a warning, a request, the right word:

"It seems to me that you only came to give me a child," she said and only now did she have the opportunity to keep the promise she had made to Lídia. Even continuing to want the child would be connecting with the future.

Otávio stared at her for a moment in alarm, without tenderness.

"But," he mumbled after a while and his voice was hesitant, timid and hoarse, "but don't you think that everything is almost over between us?—And almost since the beginning ..." he ventured.

"It'll only be over when I have a child," she repeated vague, obstinate.

Otávio opened his eyes at her, his face pale and suddenly tired under the desk lamp, where his book lay open.

"A little contrived this idea, don't you think?" he asked ironically.

She didn't notice:

"What has been between us isn't enough in itself. If I still haven't given you everything, you may call on me one day or I might miss you. Whereas after a child there will be nothing left for us but separation."

"And what about the child?" he asked. "What will the poor thing's role be in this whole wise arrangement?"

"Oh, he'll live," she answered.

"Is that all?" he said, trying sarcasm.

"What else can you do besides that?" She shot the question into the air, lightly, without waiting for a reply.

Otávio, thinking she was waiting, despite his shyness and anger at obeying her, concluded hesitantly:

"Be happy, for example."

Joana raised her eyes and looked at him from afar with surprise and a certain glee—why?—Otávio wondered frightened. He blushed as if he had made a ridiculous joke. She saw him cross and shrunken in the bottom of his chair, offended and smarting as if someone had spat in his face. Immobile, she leaned toward him nevertheless, full of pity and more than pity—she pressed her lips together, confused—a love full of tears. She closed her eyes for a moment, trying not to see him, not to want him anymore. Deep down she still could have connected with Otávio, little did he know how much. All it would have taken perhaps was to talk to him about her own fears, for example, summing up in words that feeling of shame and shyness when she called the waiter in a loud voice, everyone else heard and only he didn't. She laughed. Otávio would like to know that. She could also bond with him by telling him about her desire to flee whenever she found herself around cheerful men and women and she herself didn't know how to position herself among them and prove her body. Or perhaps she was wrong and the confession wouldn't bring them any closer. Just as when she was young she used to imagine that, if she could tell someone the "mystery of the dictionary," she would be forever connected with that person … Like this: after *l* it was useless looking up *i* … Up to *l*, the letters were chummy, as sparse as beans scattered across the kitchen table. But after *l*, they suddenly ran serious, compact and you could never find for example an easy letter such as *a* among them. She smiled, slowly unclosed her eyes and now calm, weakened, she was able to see him dispassionately.

"You know very well it's not about that. Oh, Otávio, Otávio …" she murmured after a moment, her flames suddenly revived, "what exactly is happening to us, what is happening to us?"

Otávio's voice was harsh and quick when he answered:

"You've always left me on my own."

"No …" she said startled. "It's just that everything I have can't be given. Or taken. I myself could die of thirst in my presence. Solitude is mixed up with my essence …"

"No," he repeated, obstinately, bleary-eyed. "You've always left me on my own because you wanted to, because you wanted to."

"It's not my fault," cried Joana, "believe me … It is engraved in me that solitude comes from the fact that each body irremediably has its own end, it is engraved in me that love ceases in death … My presence has always been this mark …"

"I was first drawn to you," he said sardonically, "thinking you were going to teach me something more than that. I needed," he proceeded lowering his voice, "that which I sensed in you and which you have always denied."

"No, no …" she said fragilely. "Believe me, Otávio, the truest things I know have passed through my skin, they have come to me almost treacherously … Everything I know I never learned and could never teach anyone."

They fell silent for an instant. In a flash Joana saw herself sitting next to her father, a bow in her hair, in a waiting room. Her father's hair was unkempt, he was a little dirty, sweaty, in a cheerful mood. She could feel the bow above all things. She had been playing with her feet in the dirt and had quickly pulled on her shoes without washing them and now they chafed gritty inside the leather. How could her father be nonchalant, how did he not notice that they were the most wretched, that no one even glanced at them? But she wanted to prove to everyone that she would stay like that, that the father was hers, that she would protect him, that she would never wash her feet. She saw herself sitting next to her father and didn't know what had happened an instant before the scene or an instant afterwards. Just a shadow and she withdrew to it hearing the music of confusion murmur in its depths, impalpable, blind.

"Yet," Otávio went on, "you said yourself: there is a certain moment in the joy of knowing that you can in which you overcome your own fear of death. Two people who live together," he went on in a lower voice, "seek perhaps to reach this moment. You didn't want to."

She didn't answer. Whenever she didn't answer him, he became alarmed, recalling his childhood, people were angry and he had to promise, to please, full of remorse. He remembered an old feeling of guilt towards Joana and sought to rid himself of it immediately, lest it ever burden him again. And although he knew he was going to speak out of place, he couldn't help himself:

"You're right, Joana: everything that comes to us is raw material, but there is nothing that escapes transfiguration," he began and shame immediately spread across his face at Joana's raised eyebrows. He forced himself to go on. "Don't you remember you once told me: 'today's pain will be your joy tomorrow; there is nothing that escapes transfiguration.' Don't you remember? Maybe it wasn't exactly like that ..."

"I remember."

"Well ... At the time I didn't think your words were simple. I was even angry, I suppose ..."

"I know," said Joana. "You told me that if you had a pain in your liver I would come proclaim at your feet the same useless magnificence."

"Yes, yes, that was it," said Otávio quickly, afraid. "You weren't at all intimidated, I don't think. But ... look, I don't think I told you: later I understood that there was no superfluous wealth in what you had said ... I don't think I ever confessed that to you, or did I? Look, I actually suppose that in this sentence is the truth. There is nothing that escapes transfiguration ..." He blushed. "Maybe that's the secret, maybe that's what I sensed in you ... There are certain presences that allow transfiguration."

Because she remained silent, he pushed himself once more. "You promise too much ... All the possibilities that you offer people, within themselves, with a look ... I don't know."

And just as she hadn't acted conceited or belittled when he had joked the first time about the useless magnificence, now she didn't take delight in Otávio's humility. He looked at her. Once again he hadn't known how to connect with that woman. Once again she had won.

There was silence in the room and the light and the emptiness rested on the white keys of the open piano. Something was dead, slow and true. Reconnecting the joy of living to that moment would have been pointless.

"What comes next?" muttered Otávio and this time he had succumbed to the bottom of things, he had been dragged to Joana's truth.

"I don't know," she said.

Otávio studied her. What was she mulling over, so distant? She seemed to hover in the center of something mobile, her body floating, unsupported, almost inexistent. Like when she talked about past events and when he sensed that she was lying. Joana's head drifted then light, she softly inclined her forehead, raised it, stammered, there was a solid, astute nucleus at first but afterwards everything was fluid and innocent. Inspiration guided her movements. And Otávio forgot himself as he stared at her. Anxiety ended up constricting his heart, because if he wanted to touch her he wouldn't be able to, there was an insurmountable, impalpable circle around that creature, isolating her. Bitterness gripped him then because he didn't feel her as a woman and his manly nature was rendered useless and he couldn't be any other thing but a man. In cousin Isabel's garden white roses once grew. He had often looked at them perplexed, not knowing how to have them, because in their presence his only power, that of living creature, was useless. He pressed them to his face, his lips, inhaled them. They continued trembling delicately luxuriant. If at least they had thick petals, he used to think, if at least they were hard ... if at least when they fell they smashed on the ground with a dry sound ... Feeling the flowers' growing allure invade him, like Joana's, like Joana's when she lied, he fell prey to an impotent fury: he crushed them, chewed them, destroyed them.

Looking at her now, unable to define it, that face, he wanted to reconstitute that old feeling, return to his cousin Isabel's garden.

But instead of any other thought, he suddenly understood that Joana was going to leave. Yes, he would continue, there was Lídia, the child, himself. She was going to leave, he knew it ... But what did it matter, he didn't need Joana. No, not "didn't need," but "couldn't." And suddenly he really couldn't understand how he had lived beside her for so long and he felt that after she was gone he would simply have to unite the present with that distant past, of cousin Isabel's house, of fiancée-Lídia, of his plans for a serious book, of his own tortures as warm, sweet and repugnant as an addiction, with that past merely interrupted by Joana. It would be good to rid himself of her, to see through his plan for a book on civil law. He could already see himself strolling among his things with intimacy.

But he also saw, with strange, sudden clarity, himself on an afternoon perhaps, feeling a sharp pain in his chest, wrinkling his eyes, knowing his hands were empty without looking at them. The indefinable feeling of loss when Joana left him ... She would rise up in him, not in his head like a common memory, but in the center of his body, vague and lucid, interrupting his life like the sudden pealing of a bell. He would suffer as if she were telling crazy lies, but as if he couldn't expel the hallucination and inhaled it more and more like an air that inside the body could blessedly turn into water. He would feel the open, clear space in his heart, which none of Joana's seeds had been able to cover with a forest, because she was unpossessed like future thought. Yet she was his, yes, profoundly, diffusely like a song once heard. Mine, mine, don't leave!—he implored from the depths of his being.

But he would not utter such words because he wanted her to leave, he wouldn't know what to do with Joana if she stayed. He would go back to Lídia, pregnant and wide. He slowly realized that he had chosen to renounce the most precious thing in his being, that small suffering portion that by Joana's side had managed to live. And after a moment of pain, as if he were abandoning himself, his eyes glistening with weariness, he felt the impotence of desiring something more for the future. Perplexed, he at last watched his violent, strange purification, as if he were slowly entering an inorganic world.

"Do you really want a child?" he asked because, afraid of the solitude in which he had advanced, he suddenly wanted to connect with life, to lean on Joana until he could lean on Lídia, like someone who when crossing an abyss clings to the smaller rocks until he climbs the biggest.

"We wouldn't know how to make it live ..." came Joana's voice.

"Yes, you're right ..." he said frightened. And he violently longed for Lídia's presence. To go back, go back forever. He understood that this would be his last night with Joana, the last, the last ...

"No ... maybe I'm right," Joana continued. "Maybe you don't think about any of this before having a child. You switch on a strong light, everything becomes bright and safe, you drink tea every afternoon, you embroider, above all a brighter light than this one. And the child lives. That's the truth ... so much so that you didn't fear for the life of Lídia's child ..."

Not a muscle in Otávio's face moved, his eyes did not blink. But all of him condensed and his paleness shone like a lit candle. Joana continued speaking slowly, but he didn't hear her because little by little, almost without thoughts, fury came rising up through his heavy heart, deafened his ears, clouded his eyes. What ..., anger thrashed about in him, staggering and gasping, so she knew about Lídia, about the baby ... she knew and she didn't say anything ... She was deceiving me ... — The asphyxiating load weighed deeper and deeper inside him. — She accepted my shame serenely ... she continued sleeping beside me, putting up with me ... for how long? Why? but, dear God, why?! ...

"Shameful."

Startled, Joana lifted her head quickly.

"Vile."

His swollen throat could barely contain his voice, the veins in his neck and forehead throbbed thick, gnarled, in triumph.

"It was your aunt who called you a viper. Viper, yes. Viper! Viper! Viper!"

Now he was shouting hysterically out of control. Viper. No sooner had each bellow freed itself of its convulsing source than it vibrated in the air almost cheerful. She watched him thump his fists on the desk crazed, crying with outrage. How long? Because Joana was aware, as if of distant music, that everything continued to exist and his bellows were not isolated arrows, but merged with what existed. Until suddenly exhausted and empty he sat on a chair, slowly. Face flaccid, eyes dead, he stared at a point on the ground.

The two of them sank into a solitary, calm silence. Years passed perhaps. Everything was as limpid as an eternal star and they hovered so quietly that they could feel future time rolling lucid inside their bodies with the thickness of the long past which instant by instant they had just lived.

Until the first light of dawn began to dissolve the night. In the garden the darkness frayed into a veil and the sunflowers trembled in the breeze that was starting to pick up. But the little lights still twinkled in the depths of the distance like the sea's.

The Men's Departure

THE NEXT DAY SHE RECEIVED A NOTE FROM THE MAN, saying goodbye:

"I've had to go away for a while, I had to go, they came to take me away, Joana. I'll be back, I'll be back, wait for me. You know I am nothing, I'll be back. I wouldn't even be able to see or hear if it weren't for you. If you leave me, I'll live a little longer, as long as a tiny bird can stay in the air without flapping its wings, then I'll fall, I'll fall and die. Joana. The only reason I don't die now is because I'll be back, I can't explain but I can see through you. God help me and may he help You, one and only, I'll be back. I've never talked so much to you, but please: I'm not breaking my promise, am I? I understand you so so much, everything that You need from me I have to do. God bless you, here is my Saint Christopher and Saint Thérèse medallion."

She folded the letter slowly. She remembered the man's face, over the last few days, his moist, cloudy, sick cat's eyes. And the skin around them dark and purplish, like twilight. Where had he gone? His life was certainly a mess. A mess of facts. And somehow he struck her as unconnected to these facts.

The woman who supported him, his distractedness regarding himself, like one who had no beginning and didn't expect an end ... Where had he gone? She had suffered a lot over the last few days. She should have told him, she had actually meant to, but then, preoccupied and selfish, she had forgotten.

Where had he gone? — she wondered, arms empty. The whirlwind span, span, and she was deposited back at the beginning of the road. She looked at the note where the handwriting was fine and indecisive, the sentences written with care and difficulty. She recalled her lover's face and loved his fair features delicately. She closed her eyes for a moment, smelled once more the scent that came from the dark corridors of that unexplored house, with just one room revealed, where she had known love again. The scent of old apples, sweet and old, that came from the walls, from its depths. She pictured the narrow bed that had been replaced with a wide, soft one, the cheerful shyness with which the man had opened the door that day and peered at Joana's face surprising her surprise. The little ship on the excessively green waves, almost submerged. When she half closed her eyelids the ship moved. But everything had slid over her, nothing had possessed her ... In short just a pause, a single note, weak and clear. It was she who had violated the man's soul, filled it with a light whose evil he had yet to understand. She herself had barely been touched. A pause, a light note, without resonance ...

Once again a circle of life that was closing. And there she was in Otávio's quiet, silent house, feeling his absence in each place where his objects had still existed the day before and where now there was a slightly dusty emptiness. Good thing she hadn't seen him leave. And good thing that, in those first instants, when she painfully noted his departure, she still believed she had the lover. "When she noticed Otávio's departure …?" she thought. But why lie? The one who had departed was her and Otávio knew it too.

She took off the clothes she had put on to go see the man. The woman with moist, slack lips must be suffering, alone and old in the big house. Joana didn't even know his name … She hadn't wanted to know it, she had told him: I want to know you through other sources, seek your soul along other paths; I desire nothing of your life that has passed, not even your name, not even your dreams, not even the story of your suffering; the mystery explains more than the light; you will not ask anything about me either; I am Joana, you are a body living, I am a body living, nothing more.

Oh fool, fool, perhaps you would have suffered then and loved if you'd known his name, his hopes and hurts. Truth be told the silence between them had been more perfect like that. But what was the point … Just bodies living. No, no, it was even better like that: each with a body, pushing it forward, eagerly wanting to live it. Seeking full of greed to climb over the other, asking full of shrewd and touching cowardice to exist better, better. She interrupted herself holding the dress, watchful, light. She became aware of the solitude she was in, at the center of an empty house. Otávio was with Lídia, she sensed, taking refuge with that pregnant woman, full of seeds for the world.

She went over to the window, felt cold on her bare shoulders, looked at the earth where the plants were quietly living. The globe moved and she was standing on it. Next to a window, the sky overhead, bright, infinite. There was no point taking shelter in the pain of each episode, getting angry at the things that happened, because the facts were just a big tear in her dress, the silent arrow indicating the bottom of things again, a river that dries up and reveals its naked riverbed.

The afternoon coolness gave Joana goose bumps, she couldn't think clearly—there was something in the garden that was throwing her off-center, causing her to falter ... She stayed on the alert. Something was trying to move inside her, answering, and through the dark walls of her body light, cool, old waves rose up. Almost frightened, she wanted to bring the feeling to awareness, but she kept being dragged back in a sweet swoon, by soft fingers. As if it was morning. She studied herself, suddenly alert as if she had ventured too far. Morning?

Morning. Where had she been once, on what strange, miraculous earth had she rested to now smell its perfume? Dry leaves on the moist earth. Her heart tightened slowly, opened, she didn't breathe for a moment waiting ... It was in the morning, she knew it was in the morning ... Regressing as if by a child's fragile hand, she heard, muffled as if in a dream, chickens scratching the earth. Hot, dry earth ... the clock clanging tin-dlen ... tin ... dlen ... the sun raining in tiny yellow and red roses over the houses ... Dear God, what was that if not herself? but when? no, always ...

The pink waves were darkening, the dream was slipping away. What was it that I lost? what was it that I lost? It wasn't Otávio, already far away, it wasn't her lover, the unhappy man had never existed. It occurred to her that he must have been arrested, she pushed away the thought impatient, fleeing, dashing headlong ... As if everything were partaking of the same madness, she suddenly heard a nearby rooster release its violent, solitary cry. But it's not dawn, she said trembling, running her hand across her cold forehead ... The rooster didn't know it was going to die! The rooster didn't know it was going to die!

Yes, yes: Daddy, what shall I do? Ah, she had skipped the bar of a minuet ... Yes ... the clock had clanged tin-dlen, she had risen up on tiptoes and the world had spun much more slowly at that moment. Were there flowers somewhere? and a great desire to dissolve until her ends merged with the beginnings of things. To form a single substance, rosy and mild—breathing tamely like a belly that rises and falls, rises and falls ... Or was she mistaken and that feeling was current? What there was in that long-ago moment was something green and vague, the expectation of continuity, an impatient or patient innocence? empty space ... What word could express that back then something hadn't condensed and lived more freely? Open eyes floating among yellowing leaves, white clouds and much further down the countryside rolled out, as if enveloping the earth. And now ... Maybe she had learned to speak, that was all. But the words, indissoluble, hard, floated on the surface of her sea. Before, she was the pure sea. And all that was left of the past, trickling inside her, quick and tremulous, was a little of the old water through pebbles, shadowy, cool under the trees, dead brown leaves lining the banks. Dear God, how sweetly she sank into the incomprehension of herself. And how, even more so, she was able to let herself go with the firm, soft ebb. And return. She would reunite with herself one day, without the hard, solitary words ... She would weld herself and be once again the mute brusque strong wide unmoving blind living sea. Death would connect her with childhood.

But the bars of the gate were man-made; and there they were glinting under the sun. She noticed them and in the shock of her sudden perception she was a woman again. She shuddered, lost from her dream. She wanted to return, to return. What had she been thinking about? Ah, death would connect her with childhood. Death would connect her with childhood. But now her eyes, staring outwards, had cooled. Now death was different, since the bars of the gate were man-made and since she was a woman … Death … And suddenly death was just cessation … No! she cried at herself frightened, not death.

She was running ahead of herself now, already far from Otávio and the man who had disappeared. Don't die. Because … in actual fact where was death in her?—she asked herself slowly, shrewdly. She dilated her eyes, still not believing in the question so new and full of fascination that she had allowed herself to invent. She walked over to the mirror, looked at herself—still alive! Her pale neck sprouting from delicate shoulders, still alive!—looking for herself. No, listen! listen! the beginning of death didn't exist in her! And as if crossing her body itself violently, in search, she felt a zephyr of health lift up from her interior, the whole thing opening up to breathe …

So she couldn't die, she then thought slowly. Little by little the fragile thought took a long breath, grew, became compact and solidified like a block adjusting to its contours. There was no room for another presence, for doubt. Her heart beating strong, she listened to herself attentively. She laughed out loud, a tremulous, trilling laugh. No … But it was so clear … She wouldn't die because … because she couldn't end. Yes, yes. A quick vision, of an old man, perhaps a woman, a mixture of indistinct faces in just one, shaking their head, refusing, aging. No, she told them softly from the bottom of her new truth, no … The faces turned to smoke, for she had always been. For her body had never needed anyone, it was free. For she walked through the streets. She drank water, had abolished God, the world, everything. She wouldn't die. So easy. She held out her hands not knowing what to do with them now that she knew. Perhaps caress herself, kiss herself, recognize herself full of curiosity and gratitude. No longer concerned with reasoning, it seemed so illogical to die, that she stopped now aghast, filled with terror. Eternal? Violent ... Reflections lightning-fast and bright as sparks flew every which way electrically, merging more into feelings than thoughts. She changed with no transition, skipping lightly, from plane to plane, ever higher, clearer and tenser. And with each instant she fell deeper and deeper into herself, into caverns of milky light, her breathing vibrant, full of fear and happiness at the journey, perhaps like falling in sleep. Her intuition that those moments were fragile made her move lightly afraid to touch herself, to stir up and dissolve that miracle, the tender being of light and air that was trying to live inside her.

She drifted over to the window again, breathing carefully. Immersed in such a fine, intense joy almost like the cold of ice, almost like the perception of music. Her lips began to quiver, serious. Eternal, eternal. Shining and jumbled came a succession of wide brown lands, sparkling green rivers, running with fury and melody. Glittering liquids like fires spilling inside her transparent body from huge pitchers ... She herself growing over the asphyxiated earth, dividing into thousands of living particles, full of her thinking, of her force, of her unconsciousness ... Crossing the clarity without mists lightly, walking, flying ...

A bird outside flew obliquely!

It crossed the pure air and disappeared into the density of a tree.

The silence palpitated behind it in tiny whispers. How long she had been watching it, without feeling.

Ah, so she would die.

Yes, she would indeed die. As simply as the bird had flown. She tilted her head to one side, softly like a docile madwoman: but it's easy, so easy ... it isn't even intelligent ... it is death that will come, that will come ... How many seconds had passed? One or two. Or more. The cold. She realized that by a miracle she had now become aware of those thoughts, that they were so profound that they had passed under other material, easy ones, simultaneously ... While she was living her dream, she had observed the things around her, used them mentally, nervously, as one scrunches a curtain while gazing at the landscape. She closed her eyes, sweetly serene and tired, wrapped in long gray veils. For a moment she still felt the threat of incomprehension surging up in the distant interior of her body like blood flowing. Eternity is non-being, death is immortality—they were still floating there, leftover scraps of torment. And she no longer knew what to connect them to, she was so tired.

Now the certainty of immortality had vanished forever. Once or twice more in her life—perhaps late one afternoon, in an instant of love, at the moment of death—she would have the sublime creative unconsciousness, the sharp, blind intuition that she was really immortal for all time.

The Journey

IMPOSSIBLE TO EXPLAIN. SHE WAS SLOWLY STRAYING
from that zone where things have a set shape and edges, where
everything has a solid, immutable name. She was sinking
deeper into the liquid, quiet, unfathomable region, where mists
hung as vague and cool as those of the dawn. Of dawn rising
in the countryside. On her uncle's farm she had awoken in the
middle of the night. The floorboards of the old house creaked.
From up on the first floor, floating in the dark space, she had
sunk her eyes into the earth, looking for the plants that twisted
and coiled around one another like vipers. Something blinked
in the night, watching, watching, eyes of a dog lying down, vigilant. The silence pulsed in her blood and she throbbed with it.
Then dawn broke over the fields, rosy, moist. The plants were
once again green and naive, their stalks quivering, sensitive to
gusts of wind, emerging from death. There was no longer a dog
guarding the farm, now everything was one, light, unaware.
There was a horse loose in the quiet field, the mobility of its
legs merely divined. Everything imprecise, but suddenly in imprecision she found a clearness that she had only sensed and

hadn't been able to possess entirely. Perturbed she thought: everything, everything. Words are pebbles rolling in the river. It wasn't happiness that she felt then, but what she felt was fluid, sweetly amorphous, resplendent instant, somber instant. Somber like the house that stood on the highway, covered with leafy trees and dust from the road. In it lived an old, barefooted man and two sons, big, handsome stallions. The youngest had eyes, above all eyes, he had kissed her once, one of the best kisses she had ever felt, and something rose up in the back of his eyes whenever she gave him her hand. The same hand that was now resting on the back of a chair, like a separate little body, satisfied, negligent. When she was young she used to make it dance, like a tender young lady. She had even danced it for the man who was on the run or locked up, for her lover—and fascinated and anxious he had ended up squeezing it, kissing it as if her hand alone really was a woman. Ah, she had lived a lot, the farm, the man, the waits. Whole summers, where the nights passed sleepless, leaving her pale, eyes dark. Inside insomnia, several insomnias. She had known perfumes. A smell of moist greenery, greenery illuminated by lights, where? She had stepped then in the wet earth of the flower beds, while the guard wasn't paying attention. Lights dangling from wires, swinging, like this, meditating indifferent, bandstand music, uniformed, sweaty negroes. The trees all lit up, the cold, artificial air of prostitutes. And above all there was what cannot be spoken: eyes and mouth behind the curtain watching, eyes of a dog blinking at intervals, a river rolling in silence without knowing. Also: the plants growing from seeds and dying. Also: faraway somewhere, a sparrow on a branch and someone sleeping. Everything dissolved. The farm also existed in that same instant and in that same instant the hand of the clock was moving forward, while the perplexed feeling found itself overtaken by the clock.

Inside her she felt the time lived piling up again. The feeling was floaty like the memory of a house in which one has lived. Not the house itself, but the position of the house inside her, in relation to her father pounding at the typewriter, in relation to the neighbor's yard and the late afternoon sun. Vague, far-away, mute. An instant … it was over. And she had no way of knowing if after the time lived there would be a continuation or a renewal or nothing, like a barrier. No one was stopping her from doing exactly the opposite of any of the things she was going to do: no one, nothing … she didn't have to follow her own beginning … Did it hurt or cheer her up? Nevertheless she felt that this strange freedom that had been her curse, that had never connected her even with herself, this freedom was what illuminated her matter. And she knew that her life and moments of glory came from it and that the creation of each future instant came from it.

She had survived like a still-moist microbe among the scorching-hot, dry rocks, thought Joana. On that already old afternoon (a circle of life closed, work finished), the afternoon she had received the man's note, she had chosen a new path. Not to run away, but to go. To use her father's untouched money, the inheritance abandoned until now, and roam, roam, be humble, suffer, be shaken to her core, without hopes. Above all without hopes.

She loved her choice and serenity now stroked her face, allowing past, dead moments to come to her awareness. Be one of those people without pride or shame that entrust themselves to strangers with no prior warning. That was how before death she would connect with childhood, through nudity. Lower herself at last. How can I punish myself enough, how to open myself to the world and to death?

The ship floated lightly on the sea like on gentle open hands.

She leaned over the railing on the deck and felt tenderness rising slowly, enveloping her in sadness.

On the deck the passengers were pacing back and forth, hardly able to bear the wait for supper, anxious to reunite time with time. Someone said in a doleful voice: look at the rain! The grey mist really was approaching, eyes closed. Soon they saw broad raindrops fall on the planks of the deck, the sound of needles falling, and over the water, imperceptibly piercing its surface. The wind cooled, coat collars were turned up, gazes became suddenly restless, shunning melancholy like Otávio with his fear of suffering. De profundis …

De profundis? Something wanted to speak … De profundis … Hear herself! Catch the fleeting opportunity that danced light-footedly on the verge of the abyss. De profundis. Close the doors of awareness. At first perceive corrupted water, dizzy phrases, but afterwards amidst the confusion the trickle of pure water quivering over the rough wall. De profundis. Approach carefully, allow the first waves to wash back. De profundis … She closed her eyes, but only saw penumbra. She fell deeper into her thoughts, saw a thin unmoving figure outlined in light red, the drawing made with a bloody finger on a piece of paper, when she had a scratch and her father had gone looking for iodine. In the dark of her pupils, thoughts were aligned geometrically, one superimposing the next like a honeycomb, some cells empty, shapeless, without place for reflection. Soft, grey forms, like a brain. But she didn't really see it, she tried to imagine it perhaps. De profundis. I see a dream I once had: abandoned dark stage, behind some stairs. But the minute I think "dark stage" in words, the dream is depleted and the cell is left empty. The feeling withers and is just mental. Until the words "dark stage" have lived enough in me, in my darkness, in my perfume, to the extent that they become a shadowy vision, frayed and impalpable, but behind the stairs. Then I will have a truth again, my dream. De profundis. Why doesn't whatever wants to speak come? I am ready. Close my eyes. Full of flowers that turn into roses as the beast shakes and advances towards the sun just as the vision is much faster than words, I choose the birth of the ground to … Makes no sense. De profundis, afterwards the trickle of pure water will come. I saw the snow tremble full of rosy clouds under the blue function of the viscera crawling with flies in the sun, the grey impression, the green and translucent and cold light that exists behind the clouds. Close my eyes and feel inspiration roll like a white cascade. De profundis. My God I wait for thee, God come to me, God, blossom in my breast, I am nothing and misfortune falls on my head and I only know how to use words and words lie and I continue to suffer, in the end the trickle over the dark wall, God come to me and I am joyless and my life is as dark as the starless night and God why do you not exist in me? why did you make me separate to you? God come to me, I am nothing, I am less than dust and I wait for you every day and every night, help me, I only have one life and this life slips through my fingers and travels to death serenely and I can do nothing and all I do is watch my depletion with each passing minute, I am alone in the world, those who are fond of me don't know me, those who know me fear me and I am small and poor, I won't know I existed in a few years' time, all that is left for me to live is little and yet all that is left for me to live will remain untouched and useless, why do you not take pity on me? me who is nothing, give me what I need, God, give me what I need and I don't know what that is, my desolation is as deep as a well and I am not mistaken as far as myself and others are concerned, come to me in misfortune and misfortune is today, misfortune is always, I kiss your feet and the dust of your feet, I want to dissolve in tears, from the depths I call thee, come to my aid for I have not sinned, from the depths I call thee and you do not answer and my desperation is dry like the desert sands and my perplexity suffocates me, humiliates me, God, this pride to be alive gags me, I am nothing, from the depths I call thee, from the depths I call thee from the depths I call thee from the depths I call thee …

By now her thoughts had solidified and she was breathing like a sick person who had passed through the great danger. Something was still spluttering inside her, but her weariness was great, it tranquilized her face in a smooth, empty-eyed mask. From the depths the final surrender. The end …

But from the depths as an answer, yes as an answer, revived by the air that still entered her body, the flame rose up burning lucid and pure … From the somber depths the merciless impulse ablaze, life rising up again formless, audacious, miserable. A dry sob as if she had been shaken, joy beaming in her chest intense, unbearable, oh the whirlwind. Above all that constant movement at the bottom of her being was becoming clearer — now it was growing and vibrating. That movement of something alive seeking to break out of the water and breathe. Also like flying, yes like flying … walking on the beach and receiving the wind in her face, hair fluttering, glory over the mountain … Rising, rising, her body opening to the air, surrendering to the blind palpitation of her own blood, crystalline, tinkling notes, sparkling in her soul … There was still no disenchantment faced with her own mysteries, oh God, God. God, come to me not to save me, it would seem that salvation is in me, but to muffle me with your heavy hand, with punishment, with death, because I am impotent and afraid to deliver the little blow that will turn all of my body into this center that longs to breathe and which rises, rises ... the same impulse as the tide and the genesis, the genesis! the little touch that in the crazy man allows only crazy thoughts to live, the luminous wound growing, floating, dominating. Oh, how she harmonized with what she thought and how what she thought was grandiosely overwhelmingly fatal. I just want you, God, so that you may take me in like a dog when everything is merely solid and complete again, when the movement of emerging my head from the waters is just a memory and when inside me there is only knowledge, which has been used and is used and through it things are received and given again, oh God.

What was rising in her was not courage, she was substance alone, less than human, how could she be a hero and want to defeat things? She wasn't a woman, she existed and what she had inside her were movements lifting her always in transition. Maybe at some point she had modified with her wild force the air around her and no one would ever notice, maybe she had invented with her breathing new matter and didn't know it, merely feeling what her tiny woman's mind could never comprehend. Throngs of warm thoughts sprouted and spread through her frightened body and what mattered about them was that they concealed a vital impulse, what mattered about them was that at the very instant of their birth there was the blind, true substance creating itself, rising up, straining at the water's surface like an air bubble, almost breaking it ... She noticed that she still hadn't fallen asleep, thought she would still surely crackle on an open fire. That the long gestation of her childhood would end and from her painful immaturity her own being would burst forth, free at last, at last! No, no, I want no God, I want to be alone. And one day it will come, yes, one day the capacity as red and affirmative as it is clear and soft will come in me, one day whatever I do will be blindly surely unconsciously, standing in myself, in my truth, so entirely cast in what I do that I will be incapable of speaking, above all a day will come on which all my movement will be creation, birth, I will break all of the noes that exist in me, I will prove to myself that there is nothing to fear, that everything I am will always be where there is a woman with my beginning, I will build inside me what I am one day, with one gesture of mine my waves will rise up powerful, pure water drowning doubt, awareness, I will be strong like the soul of an animal and when I speak my words will be unthought and slow, not lightly felt, not full of yearning for humanity, not the past corrupting the future! what I say will resound fatal and whole! there will be no space in me for me to know that time, man, dimensions exist, there will be no space in me to even realize that I will be creating instant by instant, not instant by instant: always welded, because then I will live, only then will I live bigger than in my childhood, I will be as brutal and misshapen as a rock, I will be as light and vague as something felt and not understood, I will surpass myself in waves, ah, Lord, and may everything come and fall upon me, even the incomprehension of myself at certain white moments because all I have to do is comply with myself and then nothing will block my path until death-without-fear, from any struggle or rest I will rise up as strong and beautiful as a young horse.

RIO

MARCH — 1942

NOVEMBER — 1942